CITY OF PORTS

THE SHADOW OVER PORTSMOUTH BOOK 1

JEFF DECK

ALSO BY JEFF DECK

City of Games: The Shadow Over Portsmouth Book 2

The Pseudo-Chronicles of Mark Huntley

Player Choice

The Great Typo Hunt:
Two Friends Changing the World, One Correction at a Time
(with Benjamin D. Herson)

Short stories featured in:

Murder Ink 2: Sixteen More Tales of New England Newsroom Crime
(Plaidswede Publishing)

Corporate Cthulhu (Pickman's Press)

Robots & Artificial Intelligence Short Stories (Flame Tree Publishing)

CITY OF PORTS

THE SHADOW OVER PORTSMOUTH BOOK 1

JEFF DECK

City of Ports: The Shadow Over Portsmouth Book 1
by Jeff Deck

Book cover design provided by Damonza.

You'll receive a FREE book by signing up for my e-mail updates. Just go to: www.jeffdeck.com

Thank you so much for supporting this work.

Printed in the United States of America.

❋ Created with Vellum

For Cassie

"'Every City gives a Key to distinguished visitors,' Mr. Haven said. 'But the City of Portsmouth does not, because it is known as the City of the Open Door.' . . ."
— *Portsmouth Porthole,* Monday, June 29, 1925

"Freeze the worm; still the breath
Rend the belly; join life & death."
— *Anonymous verse scratched into the attic timbers of Pitt Tavern, Portsmouth, NH*

PROLOGUE

I was the one to find your body.

That night I was on patrol in Portsmouth in zone 1, the half of Islington Street farther away from downtown. I pulled alongside Officer Skip Bradley's cruiser in one of the shopping plazas on Islington, just to check in with him. He was supposed to be patrolling zone 4, downtown, but it was a slow night. No opioid ODs or noise complaints from rich fucks, at least not yet.

"Hey girl. You need anything from Street?" Skip Bradley asked me from his open window. He unbuckled his seatbelt.

"Thanks for the offer—but I'm good." I let the *girl* comment pass.

"You sure? They got them curry fries. And 'schwarma,' that's Indian too, right?"

I sighed. "No. Thanks." The prickle of anger just under my skin made me add: "You know I grew up here in New Hampshire, right?" I added a smile just to show how cool ol' Divya Allard was. No humorless battleaxe here, just another comrade in blue. But judging from Bradley's reaction, the smile must have come out all wrong.

"Yeah? So?" He'd turned truculent.

I waved him off. "Enjoy. I'll radio you if I run into any miscreants or malcontents out here." And then, just because I don't know when to shut my mouth, I added, "Shiva's blessings be upon you!"

He gave me a confused look and headed into the Street restaurant for his coffee and snack (and perhaps a *hey girl* for the hostess).

I told you enough times about the shit I had to deal with as a woman in the department, and a woman of color at that. But I loved my job. I hope you understood that, too. One day soon, I was going to make detective and show meatheads like Bradley where he could shove his *hey girl*.

I drove across the street to the opposite plaza, the one with the grocery store, and parked in a lonely spot. I was in the mood for walking. I strolled toward Brewery Lane, a quiet street in back of the plaza. That's how I happened to be there to see the person emerge from shadows between the old industrial brick buildings.

A hooded figure. Dusty red winter coat on a warm night. It approached the street from an odd angle—like it just came from the excavation site behind the Brewery Lane buildings. And it didn't seem excited to see me. It skewed its walking path away from me.

This wasn't sufficient reason for me to stop the person, whoever it was. But I did get curious.

I went the same way it came from. Between the buildings. I glanced behind me, but the figure was still walking away, not running. I kept going until I reached the excavation site. A few earth-movers stood over the hole. No foundations yet, so not much to see.

I shone my flashlight into the hole. Still, I wouldn't have spotted you if not for the flash of your engagement ring. The one I gave you, the one that matched my own. The jewel caught the light and winked, just once.

My radio crackled. "Allard. Sorry about—"

"Never mind that," I said. "Got something suspicious here. Excavation pit near the grocery plaza."

"Well, don't leave me out of the action," Bradley said. "Hold on."

I ignored his suggestion and crabwalked down the slope of dirt and rock until I reached where the wink had come from. My flashlight showed me the crumpled figure of a young woman.

As soon as I saw you, I dropped the flashlight. The lens shattered against a rock, and you and I plunged into darkness again.

My legs refused to hold me up. I banged my knee on another goddamn rock. But I wouldn't let the rebellion of my legs keep me from you. I crawled to your side. The meager moonlight showed me you were utterly still.

I tried mouth to mouth anyway. Your lips were cold.

I still couldn't accept that you were gone. I muttered *Hannah* over and over again, as if saying your name enough times would snatch you from the hereafter. I grabbed you. I shook you.

You were supposed to be the one to live forever. This just couldn't be.

"Oh my God," Bradley said. He stood at the edge of the excavation, I registered through my fog. A light shone on you and me. "Is that a body?"

"No," I said. *No, it's not a fucking lump of flesh, it's Hannah Ryder, and we're getting married as soon as we can afford a 20% down payment on a house.*

All I could say out loud was "No."

"Sure looks like one," Bradley said, coming down the slope.

In the sweep of his flashlight, I noticed the bulge in your wrist. I'd never seen it before, and I'd seen every inch of your skin. Something was not right. Something was— implanted in there. The last I'd seen you, just two days ago, your wrist had been totally normal.

I frowned at Bradley's approaching footsteps. I wanted to shield you from the oaf. People like him couldn't see you like this. Lying in a pit, twisted . . . it was indecent.

I bolted to my feet and whirled to face my colleague.

"You call it in yet?" Bradley said. He still had his stupid cup of coffee from Street, which infuriated me. His tone was placid now, as he tried to play it cool with his first real corpse. But he kept trying to shine his light around me to look at it. (At *you*.)

"No, I'll take care of it," I snapped.

Bradley read my face. For once. "Oh. Uh. You okay? You know this person?"

He hadn't gotten the chance to meet you. Most of my colleagues in the PD hadn't.

I hadn't been hiding you, not really. It was just . . . sometimes the way you talked, I got the feeling you didn't like most police officers. Or any figure of authority, for that matter. I had counted myself lucky you decided to be with me.

I was trembling. I struggled to get myself under control.

"She's my fiancée," I said.

Confusion settled over Bradley's face. "Like . . . ? Engaged?"

"Yes, you fucking twit," I said, calmly.

"But . . ." I saw Bradley recalculating certain assumptions. However, this was no time to walk him through expanding his worldview.

I turned away from him. I had to help you. Why hadn't I called it in? We needed a goddamn ambulance. I fumbled for my CB.

Bradley grabbed my arm. What he said next wasn't "I'm so sorry for your loss." Or "I can't imagine what you're going through right now." No, it was:

"Maybe you shouldn't be the one to handle this."

I let go of the CB. I rounded on my fellow officer and I socked him in the jaw.

That was, of course, the beginning of my fall.

Bradley reeled. I packed a good punch. His hand flew to his face and he spat muffled words at me. *Crazy bitch?* Hard to tell with his jaw all janked.

I radioed the incident in. I didn't refer to you as a "body." It was an ongoing emergency: you had to still be alive.

The image of that hooded figure now popped into my head. He or she had come from the direction of this excavation. I gave a vague description to dispatch, a description that would help no one.

Bradley, still holding his jaw, moved a safe distance away and watched me. I'd have to answer for assaulting a fellow officer. But the anger didn't go away at the thought of consequences. Instead, it settled over me and clouded my eyes and my brain. I was no longer Divya Allard. I was just anger.

Time stretched and warped. Those couple of minutes turned into a year of just standing there. When the ambulance arrived and the paramedics scooted down into the pit, I screamed at them for being late. Didn't they know a life hung in the balance?

Of course their first sight of you gave them all the information they needed. But they were professionals. They didn't tell me to fuck off. They went through their duties to determine beyond a doubt that you, Hannah Ryder, were in fact a corpse.

Then the rest of the cast arrived. Medical examiner; that grizzled reporter from the *Portsmouth Porthole,* Eric Kuhn; other cops. Plus a special bonus: the chief of police himself, Henry Akerman.

We exchanged only a few words, and Akerman only took one look at Bradley rubbing his jaw, before he booted me from the scene. I didn't put up much of a fight—I still had enough reason in my head to recognize that everyone must do the job they're paid to do.

However, that didn't mean I gave up on the case myself.

Case was the word I needed. The only way to quiet the screaming in my head during my paid "wellness" leave was to think about your death as a puzzle to solve. So I went on my own special investigation into your death.

At first it was easy. All I had to do was lean on your mom, your co-workers and close friends, your boss, etc. These were people I already had a relationship with, thus I had plenty of cover to speak with them during this "tragic time."

Remember how I tried to be the Cool Partner about your frequent and inexplicable little field trips? There was only that one time, four or five beers in at the Coat of Arms, when I joked about slipping a GPS tracker in your pocket. And the way you flipped out in response, I never made a "joke" like that again . . . hey, everyone needs their space. Right? I'd been determined not to be clingy.

But now I needed to know more. Where had you been those last two days? Who had you been associating with?

Through those conversations, I glimpsed dimensions of you that I hadn't known. I'd thought you never even voted; I had no clue you once belonged to the Northeast Federation of Anarchist Communists, or that such a political party even existed. And you never told me about the ghost whose presence you thought you felt on the basement stairs of your Uncle Jacob's house, or that loony expedition to Sedona, Arizona, that you apparently joined, to seek out an interdimensional gateway among the red rocks (I hope you got a refund). But all of these anecdotes were small threads, nothing I could tug on.

And had you known anyone with a red winter coat? I got nowhere with that, either.

People clammed up as I pressed harder. I became fixated on the idea that the mysterious implant in your wrist was important. Especially since nobody else seemed to have noticed it. It wasn't mentioned in Bradley's investigation report. Nor did it appear in any of the media coverage of your death.

Akerman got wind of my questions. That was when he suspended me from active duty and prohibited me from asking any more questions about your case. I sank into isolation.

But I didn't stop digging. I just took more caution.

Nobody could tell me anything about the implant. I asked Kuhn, the *Porthole* reporter who covered the story, if he saw it. He said that he hadn't. Lies. How could he not have seen it?

Even in my grief-stricken madness, I knew better than to ask Akerman or the other brass about the implant. Its total disappearance was too convenient. Someone was hiding something from me.

Skip Bradley was a different story. Bradley, who'd

considered filing an assault and battery lawsuit against me until Akerman convinced him not to embarrass the department, had been there. He must have seen *it*.

I tracked Bradley's address down without much difficulty. Like many of the Portsmouth cops, he couldn't afford to live in the city. Bradley lived alone in an apartment in Stratham, a one-horse town off Route 33.

One night I showed up at the apartment. At the second knock, Bradley showed his face.

"Al . . . Divya," he said, forcing a smile. "What a pleasure to see you. I was actually about to go to bed, though, so . . ."

He didn't shut the door in my face, though it was clear he wanted to. I realized that Skip Bradley was actually afraid of me: his fellow officer, seven inches shorter and at least seventy pounds lighter than him. Little old Allard. I almost laughed.

"Give me only a moment," I said. "I'd like to discuss that implant in Hannah's wrist. Then I'll be out of your hair. What do you say?"

Bradley neglected to respond promptly, so I pushed past him and let myself in. I entered a small kitchen. No dirty dishes or spilled food, but a funk hung in the air. *Hey girl.* I wrinkled my nose.

"I didn't invite you in, Allard. This is a bad time."

"Hey, it was a bad time for my fiancée to die, now that you mention it," I said. Bradley flinched, and I pressed on: "Just tell me one thing, Skip. Why didn't you mention the implant in your report?"

"What implant?" he said, his eyes flickering. "What the fuck do you keep talking about, what implant?"

I advanced on him. "In. Her. Wrist. I know you saw it. You were there. Did it mean anything to you?"

"I didn't see any implant. It's time for you to go, Allard. I'm gonna get Akerman on the line."

Bradley reached for his cell phone on the kitchen table, but I stepped in the way and slapped the phone into the next room.

"Oh, what are you gonna do now?" he said, bitterly. "Hit me again? You're a real fuckin' hero, you know that? I'm sorry about your friend, but Jesus, show a little respect to a man in his own home."

"Fuck you," I said. I grasped for my control, which was sliding away. I didn't *want* to beat on Bradley again. He wasn't the one who killed you. And he wasn't the one making decisions about what information belonged in the police report, or at least I thought not. But right then he was in my way. "Did Akerman tell you to leave it out?"

"I didn't see no implant," he said again. His eyes slid away from me. Lying.

I took him by surprise with a sudden thrust of my foot behind his legs, followed quickly by shoving him hard against the chest. It was the only way for someone my size to reliably knock over someone his size, and it worked. Bradley crashed down.

"Let me refresh your fucking memory," I said, and I pulled my gun on him.

He went flour-faced. Yep, now he was taking me seriously. He raised his hands even though he was on his back on the kitchen floor. "Allard, no! You crazy bitch, put your weapon down!"

"*The implant!*" I screamed. "You *saw* it, didn't you?!"

He was looking death down its black barrel. "Yes," he groaned. "Weird fuckin' thing. Don't know what kind of idiot would mess up their own body like that." His eyes flicked fearfully at me. "Um."

"And why did you not mention it in your report?"

"Chief told me not to."

"Why?"

He stammered. "I-I—"

"Hey girl," I said, "don't fuck with me." I slammed my knee down into his belly and shoved the gun up against his forehead. A dangerous move—if he believed at all that I would hesitate to shoot, this would be his opportunity to smack the gun away and physically overpower me.

But no. In that moment, Skip Bradley was fully convinced that I would kill him. And in truth, I myself no longer knew that I wouldn't.

I heard a loud report and flinched. Then I realized what I had taken for the sound of a gunshot was actually my colleague letting out a terrified fart. Any second now he would piss all over me.

"I don't know," he whispered, his voice trembling. "Above my head. Ask him."

I got off Bradley in a hurry, abruptly filled with shame and disgust at myself. What a sordid scene this made, and Bradley's bachelor standard of cleanliness was only the smallest part of it. I'd just scared a man half to death, merely to confirm something I already suspected. A man who'd baldly lied to a grieving woman, but still.

"You're gonna burn for this," he said wildly, pointing an accusing finger at me. "I'm gonna tell Chief everything."

"Not if I tell him first," I said. "Be seeing you, Skip." And I left his apartment. He didn't follow me.

Back in the clear and quiet night, I realized that the implant wasn't just a piece of the mystery. It was the key to it. And I knew where my next stop needed to be. Now I only had to decide whether continuing to chase the truth was worth risking my job.

You were gone. Even if I uncovered exactly what happened, it wouldn't bring you back from the dead. You were gone, and I needed this job.

I loved my job. I was going to make detective someday soon.

Right. I got in my car, cruised down the nearly empty Route 33. By the time I got back to Portsmouth, I'd decided that the whole police department could go fuck itself with a fishing rod. I parked in front of the Portsmouth police station. Akerman would be there. He didn't know I was coming.

I was going to find out what happened, and I didn't care what the cost would be.

ll that was then. This is now.

I walk out the ornate doors of Jacobi Investment Associates, Mr. Baldini's farewell echoing in my ears. I've just closed out another riveting day working security. It's a little after four in the afternoon, and I can't wait to get home and take off my monkey suit.

What was the highlight of today, you ask? Catching a kid before he could tag the building with graffiti? That's a contender, I suppose. But what brings me the most joy is figuring out which of the rich banker fucks are cheating on their wives.

Fuck #1, his tell is wearing the "backup suit" he keeps in his office. How do I know it's a backup? It's less pressed than his usual suits.

Fuck #2, he keeps a different phone at work. Smart guy. Most people wouldn't notice the difference between the phone he's carrying in the morning and the one he's using on his lunch break. I do.

And Fuck #3? No new clothes or phone. Just a spring in his step and a nervous quality in his eyes. Subtle. I'm not dead certain on this one, but my hunches rarely let me down.

I need to wash off the workday with sunshine. I walk up the curve of Bow Street, passing flocks of pre-summer tourists drawn to the city's fine waterfront dining. The Piscataqua glitters where I can see it, but most of the view from the street is blocked by the restaurants, shops, and expensive condos. Pay to view.

At the top of the hill sits an old church with a raised cemetery. From the sidewalk I can see the vaults built into the underside of the cemetery. I wonder, if I pulled out one of the entombed dead and somehow resurrected him, what he would say, looking at the city now. Would there be anything he recognized after hundreds of years besides the river itself?

You know he'd start by asking who let this brown woman carry a weapon and wear pants.

Yeah, some changes were definitely for the better. I pass the remains of the Memorial Bridge. Until the crews are done replacing the old rotting structure with a 21st-century version, locals need to take either a boat or nearby I-95 to get to Maine. Badger's Island looks tantalizingly close. But the swift tide of the Piscataqua would yank even the strongest swimmer away and under.

Cheerful thoughts today.

A crowd is gathered in front of the new, ugly brick edifice known as Seafare Estates. Great for those who can afford a $700K condo, but for the rest of us it just means a blocked view of the water from State Street now as well. An elegantly coiffed woman is speaking at a podium in front of the "Estates;" as I get closer, I recognize Councilor Grace Stone in mid-blather. She's the assistant mayor, but that's only because she received a few votes less than Mayor

Gantry in the last city council election. Stone holds the most de facto power on the council. A banner below her proclaims Portsmouth's recently revamped slogan: "A Little Bit Enormous."

"We are so, so fortunate to welcome Seafare Estates into our community, thanks to the fine efforts of Vauxhall Architects and the vision of Blue Coastal Realty," Councilor Stone says. "It is projects like these that attract job creators to our local economy. And now, as the Estates open, with fully half of their units presold, I would like to congratulate Portsmouth's newest residents for deciding to call this place home. I think they'll all agree that for a small city, we're 'a little bit enormous,' isn't that right?"

Tepid applause issues from the crowd, which consists mostly of wealthy people curious about their new neighbors. At the crowd's edge slouches a bored-looking reporter for the *Portsmouth Porthole,* a woman whose name I don't remember. (I'm just glad it's not Eric Kuhn, the one who pitilessly chronicled my downfall last year.) Several of my former colleagues from the Portsmouth PD ring the crowd to keep order.

I shake my head. I don't plan on sticking around to watch the big fish in our little pond nibble on each others' tails. Plus I'd rather not give my old co-workers an opportunity to mock former Officer Allard for how far she's fallen. I'm still wearing my JIA security uniform, after all.

"*Save our city!*"

An electronic squeal and a rush of static accompany this announcement. I spot a small band of protesters approaching the unveiling from my side of the crowd. They wear t-shirts over their long sleeves that say "3P"—as I recall, it stands for Power to the People of Portsmouth. Members often referred to as 3Peters. At their head marches an athletic young woman with a bullhorn; her voice drowns out the councilor's.

"*Affordable housing now!*"

The rest of the protesters echo her with a chant: "Save our city! Affordable housing *now!*"

I find myself automatically moving toward them. I don't know why, exactly. It's not like I'm a cop anymore. The only thing I guard these days is that investor building stuffed with rich bastards. But I've got a bad itch about this situation, and I don't ignore my instincts.

One of the cops has gotten there ahead of me, a rough-neck named Lewis. He blocks the woman and her cohorts from getting any closer. Meanwhile, Councilor Stone has chosen, maybe unwisely, to engage the 3Peters.

"The city of Portsmouth is committed to ensuring that all strata of our society have a place to live," she says into the mic.

"Well, this 'stratum' right here can't afford shit!" the lead protester says, leaning on the last word, which echoes through the well-to-do crowd. They wrinkle their noses. "Regular people are getting priced out of town, but all you care about is building more condos for the rich! The rest of us can't even see the waterfront anymore!"

Officer Vin Lewis snatches the bullhorn out of the woman's hand. "That's enough!" he says. "You don't have a permit to demonstrate, kids, so beat it."

"Beautiful Prescott Park has a lovely view of the water and is *right next to us*," says Stone in exasperation, contin-uing the argument even though the protester can no longer answer her.

It's true about the park, but right now I'm focused on the woman making a hard grab for her bullhorn. Officer Lewis whisks it out of reach and then says to another cop nearby, "She just tried to assault me! You saw that, right?"

The other cop grunts, noncommittal. I don't recognize him. Could be my replacement.

I recognize the spark of violence, about to be lit by anger. I know it well. I interpose myself between the protester and Lewis.

"Hey, buddy," I say to the latter. "How's the beat? Station coffee still taste like medical waste?"

Lewis's eyes open wide at the sight of me. "Allard! You'd better get the fuck out of my way."

"Why don't you give me the bullhorn, Lewis?" I say. "I'll give it back to this nice lady at a safe distance."

"Fuck you, I'll have you too for interfering with an arrest!"

The other cop, the newish guy, breaks in. He doesn't know me or my history. He only knows that Lewis is behaving like a bully to a rent-a-cop in full view of a sizable crowd with the media close by. Not to mention the cops' own boss, a city councilor, staring down at them.

"Come on, Lewis, step off," he says. "This don't look good."

Lewis turns and snaps at his colleague. I take the opportunity to lock eyes with the lead protester. I struggle not to get lost in those emerald-green depths. She's in her mid-twenties, with short dark-blonde hair framing her face and milk-white skin. She looks muscular enough to take Lewis in a fair fight, which this wouldn't be. She's angry, but not beyond reason.

"You've made your point," I say to her. "Do you really need to get beaten up by a uniform too?"

"People should know the truth about our boys in blue," she growls. But she does step back.

With that, the tension drains out of the situation. I sense the other protesters reassessing what they're willing to do—and what they've already done. This'll be in the *Porthole* for sure tomorrow. That's a win for them.

"Get them out of here," says Councilor Stone, which would have, I imagine, touched off the explosion if the spark had remained. But now the lead protester turns her back on the cops and walks away before they can manhandle her, and the rest of the 3Peters follow suit.

Lewis tosses the bullhorn in the street. It cracks on impact. I scoop up the bullhorn and stride after the protesters.

I catch up with the young woman and hand her the bullhorn. "Think you forgot something," I say.

She scowls at me, but she accepts it. "Didn't think you'd be on their side."

"I'm not on anyone's side," I say. Then I pause. "You know me, huh."

Her green gaze confirms it. Yep, I'm a local celebrity for all the wrong reasons.

"If you're looking for an autograph, I hope you brought your own pen," I say.

A smile struggles to bust through her scowl, but it loses. "Anyway, thanks—I guess."

"I get it," I say. "I don't like the direction this city's taken lately either. Just don't . . ." Ah, fuck it. "There's a few cracked eggs in the Portsmouth PD. Lewis isn't the only one. Just be more careful."

"Noted," she says. Something unsettles me about this woman. She's looking right into me, breaching borders I thought couldn't be breached. I don't think I've ever been under a gaze this intense. "You take care too, Allard. Day might come when you *have* to pick a side."

Ominous. But now she joins in conversation with a couple of 3Peters nearby. Allard dismissed.

Go on home. You're too old to chase after pretty little idiots.

I obey the inner voice. I go home to my little walk-up above Piscataqua Savings Bank on Pleasant Street, I lock the rattly door, and I think about you.

I guess it's no surprise, then, when I dream about you. Again.

I'M SKIDDING to the bottom of the excavation, in the dark. I find you broken and bashed-in, lying in the debris. But this time you wipe the dirt off yourself and you stand up.

You're still dead, no question about it. Your head looks like a melon someone dropped while unloading their groceries. And your eyes are—flat. Nothing there. But you, or something else, can still make your corpse move.

And, apparently, speak.

As your bruised lips open, I flinch. It's what I've fantasized about all this time—just a few last words, anything to help me understand what happened to you. Yet suddenly I dread what you're going to say. And how you're going to sound.

The first word out of your mouth is "*Divya.*"

I hold back a scream at that rusty, broken sound. My hand goes to my service weapon, but I don't draw. The slightest outburst from me could break the dream. And I need *something* to take back with me to the waking world.

"*Come with me,*" you say. Each word is a barbed broach scraping through the flesh of your throat. It's obvious what it costs you. I nod quickly, eager for you to not have to say anything else.

You shuffle a few paces along the floor of the excavation. What I expect next is the awful spectacle of you dragging your corpse up the slope. Clambering over rocks, maybe leaving a fingernail or two behind. But you stop. Your neck creaks as your ruined face looks at me once again.

A flame bursts out of the dark. I don't know where it came from—it's not supposed to be there, not in an abandoned excavation—but it's getting bigger. It forms a ring. Like that old Johnny Cash song. Except there's something in the middle of this ring of fire: a distortion, an illusion. A stone floor with the perception of distance. Like the fire ring is a window and I'm looking onto another place.

I take a step back, forgetting that none of this can hurt me.

You grab my arm. The cold touch of your fingers, even through the sleeve of my uniform, is enough to make my jaws flap open. The biggest, most wretched scream of my life comes tumbling out.

Funny thing is, it sounds a lot like a phone.

MY EYES SNAP open and I grab for the jangling, vibrating little monster in my lap and I say in a hoarse bark, "*Hannah?*"

"Uh," says the voice on the phone. It's a man.

"Hello?" I snap. "Who the fu—"

I catch myself. Swearing is a trigger. The more I do it, the angrier I get. I don't *want* to be angry. "Who ... the heck is this?"

Heck you. Heck off. Still a little too close to the real deal.

"This is an anonymous caller," says the man. He sounds young. Awkward. His choice of words backs up the impression. "Detective, are you looking at the news online right now?"

I sit up straighter on the couch. Now sleep's cleared off, for the most part, and I can fire the old neurons like normal. "First off," I say. "This is the first time I've ever heard an anonymous caller refer to *themselves* as an 'anonymous caller.' Usually you just, you know, don't say your friggin' name and get right to the point. You're new at this?"

"Um," says the voice. Doesn't elaborate. Oh well.

"Second," I say, "I'm *not* a detective. I never made it that far. So you can just call me Allard. How does that sound?"

By now I'm tensed and fully upright, with the TV's yapping on mute and my laptop open on the coffee table. I direct my browser to portsmouthporthole.com, the New Hampshire Seacoast's source for exaggerations, slander, and the wisdom of the status quo. The big headline on the news site says: *BODY FOUND ON PEIRCE ISLAND.* The byline belongs to my least favorite journalist, Eric Kuhn.

Whoa. The corpse count in Portsmouth *has* been noticeably higher in the last year or so, but. Hmm. Usually the heroin addicts tuck themselves away in private places. Why would someone risk shooting up where the Navy patrols could trip over them, right across the water from the shipyard? Out in the cold wind from the river? No, this wasn't an OD.

"Allard," says the voice. Projecting confidence, but I hear the tremor underneath. "Are you seeing it?"

"Is this your handiwork, Anonymous Caller?" I ask.

"No," he says. "That's what we need you for. To figure out. He was—our friend."

I believe him. If this kid's a murderer, then I'm the Yoken's blue whale. But several questions must follow. "One, why don't you think the police can handle this? Two, why do you think *I* can? Three, who's 'we'? There's more than one of you?"

There's an odd noise in the background, then. A thumping or a scuffling.

"Crap," says Anonymous Caller. "Got to go. Check his wrist, Allard. You'll see the connection to Hannah. Hurry before their fixers clean up the scene. Might already be too late. Hurry, Allard. Please."

"*What* did—" I say, but the call's gone.

2

Your name. In the middle of his strange spiel.

It's a trick. If the self-proclaimed A.C. knows even the slightest thing about me, then he knows about you. The media saw to that. Also, I, in my fogged-up state, did kick off the call with your name. A.C. claimed a connection to you just to ensure I was paying attention.

I have no intention of chasing ghosts. Or re-opening doors in myself, doors that I've closed and latched and padlocked after long months with my therapist.

Yet I find myself, like a good dog, fetching my shoes. Putting them on, putting on my fine leather jacket, grabbing a penlight for good measure. And opening the heavy wooden door of my apartment, the glass rattling in the frame, and pounding down the stairs to join the Portsmouth night.

If there's a chance, however slim, to finally find out what happened to you . . .

The old adrenaline kicks in. A grey-headed couple coming down Pleasant Street gives me a wide berth. Right now my face must be wearing the look you used to call "Dog on the Hunt." Which I've finally decided is not, in fact, a compliment.

I consider backtracking to the community lot to grab my car. No, it'd be faster to jog over to Prescott Park from here and walk over the bridge. I'm only a little less in shape than I was when I wore the uniform.

Tonight plenty of people meander around the heart of the city, Market Square, as tourist season nudges in. Still not warm at night, but summer's around the corner. I head around the corner and then run down State Street. I ignore the looks from the knots of frat kids, and a little bachelorette party group in their feathers and matching t-shirts. If they're tourists, they'll be gone soon enough.

If they're locals, they'll already know me as Divya Allard, the cop that snapped. Just living up to her reputation as the town ogre, because who'd want to let that kind of title slip away?

I make good time reaching the waterfront park. I slow down as I see the blue lights strobing on Mechanic Street, in front of the bridge over to Peirce Island. By the time I reach the police blockade, I'm walking at a normal pace and my breathing is even. I see a familiar face stationed at the bridge. Familiar, but not exactly welcoming.

"Milly," I say warmly. I extend my hand.

Officer Milly Fragonard, tall and watchful, recoils from my hand. That hurts. But after everything I did to the department—I can't have expected even our friendship to survive.

"Allard, this is a crime scene," she says. Her body is as stiff as her tone. "Please step away."

She's waiting to see if I do something insane. In fact, her hand is hovering above her duty belt. I'll need to convince Milly that I've given up the insanity game.

I make a show of looking around in the darkness. "I don't see any signs of a crime here. Maybe you mean one happened on the other side of that bridge?"

"Hmm."

"So if the bridge itself wasn't involved, how about letting me walk across it? I promise I'll stop at the other end." I give her what I think is a charming smile.

Milly's expression just gets more perplexed. Her hand rests on the handle of her Sig P226.

"Step *away*," Milly says. "Don't push me, Allard."

I raise my eyebrows and my hands, and I take a few steps back. I hadn't been closer than a few yards in the first place. What was this, one psychotic breakdown and I'm out?

"I don't know what you're up to, but this has got nothing to do with you," she goes on. "Clear out of here before I notify Chief Akerman."

So she thinks dropping Akerman's name will be enough to scare me away. I *should* take this as the cue to exit, stage right, before I get arrested and lose all future chances to find out about the corpse (and, just as important, unmask Anonymous Caller).

But you know I'm a stubborn woman. The thought of leaving without landing myself even a tiny clue . . . it doesn't sit well.

So I say, "Before I go, and I am going, just tell me one thing—what did you find on his wrist?"

I feel a mean little squirt of satisfaction at the shock that crosses Milly Fragonard's face. "How did—" she starts to say, then clamps down and changes tack: "I don't know what you're talking about, Allard. Can we leave it at that, before I decide that this *does* have something to do with you?"

Anonymous Caller has just been validated.

A jovial voice rings out then: "Oh my *God!* The two Injuns, reunited! Will somebody get a goddamn picture?"

Officer Ben Ulrich enters the scene, trotting down the bridge. Suddenly the new Allard is nowhere to be found. I'm the old Allard again, with anger about to burst my seams.

I close my eyes, briefly.

My therapist Kathryn taught me all about recognizing the signs. The triggers. It took me a long time to listen, but eventually I realized that the therapy was not, in fact, bullshit. We weren't reaching back to try to figure out the "roots" of my anger. We weren't going to explore whether I was ultimately pissed at my MIA birth parents, etc. We were doing something scientific. And I respect science.

The internal bursts of emotions that I feel are involuntary. They're beyond my control. But I *can* control how I respond to them. I can replace the old destructive reactions —screaming at other people, throwing my personal belongings or using said belongings as clubs—with more measured, reasonable actions. I just need an intentional pause to step back and drive the anger train before it drives me.

So while I have a sudden mental image of grabbing Milly's sidearm, blowing out both of Ben Ulrich's kneecaps, dragging him to the bridge's edge, and then pitching him over the stone rail headfirst to sweep away in the rapid current of the Piscataqua River, the only outward tell of my anger is a slight tightening of my expression. In the darkness, it will not be noticeable. I'll call that a win.

I open my eyes and say, with as much false cheer as I can muster without gagging, "Hey, Ben! Milly here was just telling me about that weird thing on the dead guy's wrist. What do *you* think?"

As I predicted, Ulrich's *first* reaction—his own involuntary emotional response—is to join the conversation. Ulrich never met an occasion for gabbing that he didn't like (as it happens, one of the main things I loathe about him, even more so than his racism). "Oh yeah, I don't know what that gadget . . ."

He stops, then. Remembers who he's talking to, just as Milly barks out a protest or a warning or both. "Hey, wait a minute. What the fuck, Fragonard? She's not in the department anymore, or did you forget that during your girl talk?"

"I didn't say a dang thing!" Milly snaps. I feel a little bad for hanging her out to dry. "She must have some *source.*"

"Oh, a source, huh?" Ulrich says.

"Don't you have a job to do? Because tonight I have an extremely low tolerance for your—*nonsense.*"

"Sure, just keep in mind how low a tolerance the chief has for leaking information to civilians. Even if they used to wear the uniform . . ."

During this argument between my two former colleagues, I step away, just as Milly originally suggested. They notice me going, but they're too busy attacking each other to care all that much. I've gotten everything I need to know from these two. Anonymous Caller was telling the truth about the wrist thing, and Akerman was going to cover it up. Just like he did with you.

You did a lot of weird things to yourself. I guess it was one element that attracted me to you in the first place—this willingness you had to scrawl graffiti all over the temple of your body. My polar opposite. My other half, the free spirit counterbalancing Lady Uptight herself, me, unwilling even to get my ears pierced. After I met you, I still felt no desire to tat myself up or put a ring in my clit, but I finally *understood* the impulse. You saw hypocrisy everywhere you looked: misplaced ideas of purity, focused on appearance while ignoring deeper truths. You called them "false gods" of various types—false gods of the body, false gods of the street, false gods of the city. You wanted to tear them all down.

(And okay, maybe all that self-righteousness didn't make you so easy to live with. But my God (false god?), I still ache for you to be here.)

Anyway, even with all your existing tats and piercings, the wrist body mod never rang true to me. It didn't seem like something you would do. The fact that Chief Akerman had impressed upon Skip Bradley to cover it up in his report just made it seem even more important, of course.

Even after I confronted Akerman that night and blew up my own job, I still searched desperately for information on the wrist implant. All I could figure out was that it was probably a silly biometric device of the sort that exercise fanatics would use. I stalked around the fitness clubs in the area until I finally spotted someone with a similar wrist device, going into the Tenacious Trainers gym. The fact that the gym was located in the plaza close to where I'd found your body made me doubly suspicious.

But, stripped of my badge, I no longer had the freedom to investigate as I pleased. The first time I sneaked into the Tenacious Trainers gym was also the last. I quickly tripped an alarm system and triggered an arrest by my own former colleagues. Given my past record, a judge was all too happy to ban me from going within a hundred feet of the facility.

By then, I had to ask myself just what I was actually doing. Harassing fitness freaks based on a connection that could be solely circumstantial? So you'd joined a gym shortly before you died. So fucking what? I was feeling acutely unwell in my own head, and lots of people happened to be pointing that unwellness out to me. I acknowledged that . . . they had a point. That was the day when I gave up the search and started to take my therapist's advice. I couldn't imagine you wanting to see me in jail for something as stupid as a gym break-in.

Now—well, now I've got a clue to follow up on once again, and it isn't just an angry voice in my head telling me to do so. I can thank Anonymous Caller for rewarding me with a little validation.

I have to find out who the body on Peirce Island was. I check the short piece on portsmouthporthole.com for updates, but it has no info about the dead man's identity and little info about anything else.

I'll bet someone in the PD knows by now. If not Milly or Ulrich, then Akerman, and/or the reporting officer. No help in that direction—I burned all those bridges last year when I called every single one of them an "uncle-fucker." Oh, and a "cunt-licking, cat-piss-drinking colostomy bag." There's more, but you already know all my usual insults.

Fortunately, I have another avenue of approach. And if I'm not mistaken, it's almost her lunchtime.

3

"You know I can't stay long," says Figueroa. "Especially on a night like tonight. You're lucky they let me go out to grab some food."

I smile. "Must be that grande dame seniority. You're the one running the show on the night desk, yeah? Anyway, don't worry, we can order to go."

Christine Figueroa shifts in her seat and looks around nervously at the bright, eclectic space of the Friendly Toast: vintage metal signs and tacky velvet art on the walls, every server either a hipster or just dressing the part to get paid. "Yeah. It's just ... nobody *particularly* looks like they're in a hurry here."

It's true. The Friendly Toast service is notoriously slow. But I've coerced Figueroa to come to the Toast not for the peanut-butter-and-pickle pancakes, but for the covering noise, the relative privacy, and the fact that I never go here. I've chosen a table up against the wall where I'll be able to see if anyone is watching us and taking notes. Such paranoia is, oh, I don't know, maybe inappropriate at this stage of the game. But I don't know the motives of Anonymous Caller, do I? He could be trying to fuck me, and not in the nice way.

"I'm gonna get right down to business, then," I say in a low voice. "Do they have a name for the Peirce Island body?"

Figueroa nods. She writes on one of her napkins and slides it over to me. Figueroa is overweight and pallid, appropriate for a creature of the night. She works as a copy editor and page designer five nights a week for the *Portsmouth Porthole,* and that's a three to midnight shift. Sometimes even later if, say, a fire breaks out on Bow Street at 11 p.m. Wherever there's crisis, the *Porthole* is there to cover it. At least while they can afford to pay their reporters.

I take a look at the napkin: *Graham Tsoukalas.* I stuff the napkin in my pocket.

"Thank you," I say. "Thank you!"

"Eric Kuhn's on the story," Figueroa says carefully.

Right; I saw his byline. I bite my lip. Don't tell me I'll have to cross paths with *that* fucker. He dragged my name through the mud—yours too—with a series of articles last year chronicling my downfall. Nevertheless, if he has any helpful information, I'll have to be able to speak to him without throttling him.

I lean in to press the copy editor for further details, and that's when young Solomon Shrive shows up with pad in hand.

"Detective Allard!" he shouts, clearly delighted and clearly ignoring my discomfort at his decibel level. "Welcome to the Toast. And who's your buddy?"

I suppress a groan. I thought I could avoid familiar faces here, but I should have known better. Portsmouth is really a small town at heart, not a city. Still, I was almost positive my number one fan Sol didn't *work* here.

"Hey, Sol," I say. "New job?"

He nods. "Things didn't really work out at the Martingale. Or Cava. Or, uh, the fancy Mexican place on State Street. So I needed to lower my standards a little, just for the time being. I'm sure I'll be back among the upscale crowd in no time." Sol sketches a bow as he says, "*Thank* you, m'lady, *thank* you, sir," and he knocks a glass ketchup bottle off our table. He's in luck this time; it just bounces a couple of times on the parquet floor. He doesn't trouble himself to pick it up.

"Listen, we already have a server," I say. "That nice girl Rose with the bar in her nose. You don't want to encroach on her territory this early in your new career, right?"

Sol tips me a wink. "Absolutely right, Detective. I will leave you to continue speaking with this suspect."

"Suspect?" Figueroa says. "I'm—"

"Just a friend," I finish, "and I'm not a detective, Sol. Let's catch up later."

The young man nods, but he's slow to walk away. Only when another customer calls out, "Excuse me, sir? Excuse me? Sir?" does Sol return to his section of the floor.

I first met Sol while on duty: the night he overdosed on opioids. I saved his life, in fact, with a dose of Narcan. It was early in my career, when I cared a little too much about the ne'er-do-wells I met on the streets. I visited Sol occasionally during my off-hours, introduced him to the local Narcotic Anonymous folks. Even played wingwoman for him one night on a field trip to Ogunquit (Jonathan's, but sadly for Sol, none of the studs were biting at his lure). When I went on my rampage after you died, Sol was the only person who had my back. Even at my craziest.

So don't get me wrong. I like the guy. Bit of a naïf for sticking by me, but sweet. He's worked hard to recover from his addiction. He'll make a great partner for some lucky

man someday. *However*, Sol can keep a secret about as well
as a leaky gundalow can float. I need him far, far from the
radius of my investigation.

*Is that what I'm calling it now? An "investigation?" Trying on
the detective hat after all, dear old Div?*

"No!" I say, and Figueroa starts. "Sorry."

Figueroa sits up. "Here comes Rose with our boxes. I'm
sorry, Divya, I have to bounce. Matt will have my head if my
ass isn't reading galleys ten minutes from now."

"The journalist's sorry lot," I say. "Remind me never to
ask what they're actually paying you, Christine. Hey . . .
before you go, can you tell me *anything* else about,
mmm, G?"

She casts a wary look at me. "His folks live out on
Thornton Street. I think he was still living with them. That's
all I can really say. Eavesdropping only got me so far, with
the newsroom locked down." She grabs her box from the
server and gets up from the table, shrugs on her coat.

"What do you mean, locked down?"

Christine Figueroa looks truly apprehensive now. But
the chatter of the other customers in the Friendly Toast
provides enough covering noise to give her confidence.
"Your old boss stopped by earlier tonight. Chief Akerman.
He had a meeting with Matt behind closed doors. Afterward, Matt told us all to walk lightly. To not trust any
sources of information except for the police."

"That's odd," I say. "Your newsroom ever operate that
way before? On the PD's leash?"

"Used to not be that way," Figueroa mutters. "Used to be
a real paper. But lately . . . Fuck, I've said too much. Bye,
Divya. Let's have a real meal soon." And with that,
she's gone.

I clutch my own styrofoam box but leave it closed,

chewing on her parting words instead. Akerman actually going into the newspaper offices to tell them what to print and what not to. I'd think any executive editor worth his salt would be shitting a brick—a great salty brick—at the gall of a cop who'd do that, even the local captain of the blue.

Had Akerman scared him?

I shake my head. Not relevant. At least, not yet. The *Portsmouth Porthole*'s editorial independence would have to be explored some other time. Right now I have to pay a visit to the Tsoukalas house.

I'll just drive by slowly, I tell myself. *I won't barge in or ask them any questions.* I wouldn't want to take that next step into actually interfering with an active investigation, now, would I? Kathryn would be so disappointed. She'd call it backsliding. She'd call it letting my emotions rather than my thoughts dictate my behaviors.

Maybe you'd be disappointed, too.

Or maybe you'd want me to uncover just what the fuck happened tonight, if it has even a remote connection to your death.

I'VE STILL GOT Figueroa's words ringing in my ears as I arrive at Thornton Street, where the Tsoukalas family lives. I'm tempted to dwell on the possibility of conspiracy in the Portsmouth police department, just based on Akerman barging in and making dictates on the newspaper's content. After all, I didn't hesitate to draw those kinds of crazy lines last year. The PD's dismissal of the investigation just seemed too . . . quick, convenient.

Then again, that was also when I was going out of my

head. I don't want to revisit the Land of the Mad anytime soon.

I park well away from the Tsoukalas house. I'm still not sure if I'm going to cross any ethical lines—like, say, pretending I'm still on active duty with the Portsmouth PD. Nah, honesty will be the best policy. I know this little adventure will come back and bite me in the ass *somehow*—but honesty will make the bite less painful.

I march up to the front door of the Tsoukalas house. The shades in the first floor are open. I see a group of people gathered in the living room. Many of them are crying and hugging each other. Guess the word already got over here. I wonder if I've actually managed to beat the Portsmouth PD visiting the family, though.

Okay. I've got to summon that old charm that I used to practice in front of a mirror. Let the record state that Divya Allard can be likable when she needs to be. I wasn't a complete disaster at witness interviews back in the day.

"I'm so sorry for your loss . . ." I mumble to myself as I ring the bell.

It takes a minute for the door to open. A grey-haired woman, her face set in hard lines, raises her chin to challenge me. Her eyes are dry. "Yes? Who are you?"

"Ma'am, I'm Divya Allard," I say. "I'm investigating the truth behind your son's death."

"Are you with the—" the woman says, and then stops. "No. I know you. You're that cop that went insane last year when your girlfriend died. Lost your job, didn't you?"

"I did," I say. I smile. Good old painful honesty. More pain now, less later. "Thanks for remembering me. This is actually a private investigation I'm conducting—"

"We've already talked with the police," the woman says.

"I'd rather leave my son's death to the hands of the professionals, if you don't mind. Good night, Miss Allard." She starts to close the door.

I jam my foot in the door. Still smiling to show I'm not threatening, just a woman of very firm mind. "Sorry, wait," I say quickly. "I believe your son's death and my fiancée's death are connected. In a way the police department may not be ready to acknowledge. May I come in, please?"

Mrs. Tsoukalas gives me a hard, thoughtful stare. Then, finally, she says, "Come in. But you may only talk to me. We're having a—difficult time tonight. And one of your old colleagues has upset everyone enough with his questions." She opens the door grudgingly.

I come in, wondering whose ham-fisted approach I can thank for setting me up so poorly. Was it Prince? Bradley? Whoever he was, I hope he isn't coming back anytime soon.

"Let me just say first that I'm so sorry for your loss," I say to Mrs. Tsoukalas as we stand in the foyer. It's a nice, cozy house, with cheerful watercolors on the walls and a fine carved wooden staircase leading upstairs. Graham had it good. "I don't know what it's like to lose a son, but I know—"

"Let's cut to the chase," says Mrs. Tsoukalas. Still dry-eyed. Toughness is the strategy she's selected to cope. I have a feeling she's the boss in this family. "Do you have any new information? All the Portsmouth police have told us is that Graham is dead, and that he was found on Peirce Island."

"I'm still working from limited information myself," I say carefully. "I got an anonymous call from someone wanting me to look into the matter. They told me Graham had something implanted in his wrist—a gadget of some sort. My fiancée, Hannah, had the same thing in *her* wrist. I'm pretty sure that means they both belonged to the Tenacious Trainers gym."

Mrs. Tsoukalas looks interested. "An anonymous call. Very cloak and dagger, this business, and very unlike my son. You're right: the wrist implant was a health monitor. Some of the Tenacious Trainers use them for motivation during their workouts. You say you're only pretty sure your girlfriend was a gym member? I'm surprised you didn't know for certain."

"She was hiding a thing or two from me. Which made investigating her death difficult . . . Mrs. Tsoukalas, can I take a quick look in your son's room? I'm not in the mind to snoop. I just need a better idea of what Graham was like."

A tall grey-haired man comes in from the family gathering in the adjacent room. His face is haggard and his eyes are wet from weeping. "Vera," he says, "is everything all right? Who is this?"

"Joe, this is Indira Allard," says Mrs. Tsoukalas. "She's no longer with the police force, but she currently helps them with special investigations when they need a hand, isn't that right?"

"That's right," I say. I'm so grateful for her covering for me that I don't bother to correct her version of my name. The fewer people I have to talk to here tonight, the better. I may not have much time.

"Well, I wish you all the luck in the world with your investigation," Mr. Tsoukalas says. "If *someone* is responsible for Graham's death—if there's a person or people to blame —I would love to know about it. Believe me."

Mrs. Tsoukalas breaks in before I can answer. "Don't worry about all that now, dear," she says. "I'll help Indira find what she needs. Why don't you go back to consoling the rest of the family? Aunt Olivia needs a minder so she doesn't fall over. Again."

Her husband nods hurriedly, eager to please. He shuffles

back into the living room, to be greeted by a chorus of half-audible questions.

I'm half-expecting Mrs. Tsoukalas to kick me out. Instead, she steps onto the stairs and turns to me with an irritated expression. "Well? You wanted to see his room?"

"Yes, thank you so much," I say, and I follow her up.

The door at the right side of the landing leads into Graham Tsoukalas's room. At first glance, it looks like the normal abode of a twenty-year-old guy. Computer on the desk. Posters on the walls. Bookcase full of books. Everything in tidy order. I crouch down by the bookcase and note the titles by Kant, Kierkegaard, Locke.

"Philosophy major?" I ask.

"Yeah, in spite of our pushing him in a more, uh, practical direction," Mrs. Tsoukalas says. "But hey, he's paying for—" a pause here— "he was paying for his own education, so we didn't stand in his way. He loved to ask those larger questions. What's it all about? What constitutes truly moral behavior? Quiet kid, you know, a great bore at parties, but very thoughtful. We hoped he'd crack open some of life's mysteries when he got older and clue us in."

I hold back the urge to say *I'm sorry* again—during my time on the force, I learned just how useless those words are. Instead, I look more around the room. The computer would be the obvious place for clues, but it's password-locked. "You don't happen to know the . . ."

"No," Mrs. Tsoukalas says. "We weren't those kind of parents. At least not once he was old enough to be trusted."

I'm sure the Portsmouth PD will be able to get into Graham's system. But I don't have the resources or time that they do. I'll just have to gather my own clues the old-fashioned way. I absently open the top drawer of Graham's desk, dig around in the pens and rogue paper clips, and find a burned DVD. It says: *Backup.*

Backup what? Homework videos? Graham's favorite exercise routines? Let's dare to dream and say a backup of Graham's video suicide note, or a secret video confession about the one person he thinks is out to kill him. Unlikely, but. Hmm. There's a small TV in the corner with a DVD player. "Is it okay if I . . .?"

"Be my guest," says Mrs. Tsoukalas, not smiling.

I go over to the DVD player and pop *Backup* into it. I turn on the TV. Then I immediately regret what I've done.

A young couple appears on the screen, a white man and woman. They are naked. The man is taking the woman from behind. I can't see either of their faces. The woman is slender and wispy with pale blonde hair; the man is broadly built, like a football player, and sporting a tight ass. This is not a professional-grade video; this is amateur dorm-room porn.

Another young man enters the frame now. Also naked. He's holding his erect dick, but that's not what I'm focusing on: it's the face. His face matches the one in the family photos in the foyer downstairs. This is Graham Tsoukalas. With a quick glance at the camera, Graham sticks himself in the girl's mouth.

I hurry to turn off the TV. I should have done it thirty seconds ago, with Mrs. Tsoukalas standing right here. But damn me, I just had to see if this was a clue.

Now I know. It's a pretty big fucking clue, all right.

"I'm so sorry," I sputter at Graham's mother. "I had no idea what was . . ."

She waves a hand at me. "It's—it's fine. We're all grownups here. I know you're just as shocked as I am right now." Mrs. Tsoukalas's face is still calm and composed, though the tightness in her voice belies the effect. She looks away from me.

Much as I'd rather change topics, I have to ask. "Mrs. Tsoukalas. Do you—uh—have any idea who the other two people were in the video?"

She sighs. "Yes. I think I do. They've been over here a few times. Wallace and Neria. That's N-E-R-I-A for the latter. I don't remember their last names."

"You don't happen to know where they live, do you? Were they also students at Great Bay?"

"I know they were students, but I'm not sure about—" She breaks off, listening. I heard it too. We go to the window and peek behind the curtains.

A police car has just pulled up. And Officer Skip Bradley, jackhole par excellence, is getting out.

Bradley couldn't have been less helpful when I found you. I'm utterly unsurprised at his clumsiness in handling the grieving Tsoukalases tonight. Given our history, he's the one of the last cops I'd prefer to find me here at the victim's house.

"Shit," I say. "My old colleague may be unhappy to see me."

Mrs. Tsoukalas frowns. Then, thank God, she says, "There's another way out. But you'll have to be careful. I only ask that you do me a favor in return." She ejects the DVD and returns it to its case, then hands it to me.

"Please keep this out of the police's hands," she says. "I'm —fine with whatever Graham chose to do in his spare time. I remember what college was like. But I *refuse* to let this video wind up as fodder for the *Portsmouth Porthole* or, God forbid, the TV news. You know what they do. How they love the lurid little details."

"I do know," I say, and I put the DVD in my jacket pocket.

Mrs. Tsoukalas guides me toward a window at the end of the hallway. She opens it and I take a peek out. Not exactly a back staircase out of the house. There's a lower roof over-hanging a back porch. If I climb out onto it and lower myself from the edge, I may be able to drop on the ground with a minimum of broken limbs.

I hear the door open downstairs. The husband, Joe Tsoukalas, says: "Officer Bradley. Thanks for coming back. Your special contractor colleague Indira is upstairs with my wife—would you care to go up there as well?"

Fuck. I forget my reservations and scramble out the window and onto the roof. It's more slippery than I was expecting. I try to take the roof at a crawl—but I end up skidding, fast. In desperation, I grab a nearby tree branch overhanging the roof.

The slim branch breaks. I'm back on my way down.

I fumble and grab for the roof edge as I go over it. Some-how, I do get a hold, grasping painfully with the fingers of one hand, and I slam into the side of the house, making someone inside gasp. From the sound, I'm pretty sure I cracked a window. I lose my grip and fall backwards into a row of bushes just below me. It's a short fall. But I could have hoped for less spiky plants to break that fall.

Not the most dignified start to my investigation.

It only takes a moment to extricate myself from the bushes, and then I'm running. I wonder if Bradley has had the sense to come back downstairs yet. I decide rather than heading straight for the front of the house, to circle around the other side first. I can always follow some circuitous route back to my car later on.

As I round the corner, I run right into Officer Skip Bradley. Both of us fall to the ground.

Bradley's the one on top. He vaults upward. His piggish features glare with hatred down at me. I start to get up, but Bradley pulls his service weapon out and points it at me, screaming, "*Stay on the ground!*"

4

I t looks like my investigation is over. I give a brief thought to how I've failed you already. Again. And just when I had the hint of a lead. One dead college student, two Tenacious Trainer memberships, a threesome...

"You're under arrest for impersonating a police officer, dirtbag!" Bradley shouts at me. He's really taking this personally. I happen to take it personally too—it's a false accusation, after all. I *haven't* impersonated a police officer. Okay, so I let a slight misunderstanding transmit from Mrs. Tsoukalas from Mr. Tsoukalas, but I never actually said I was still a cop. These details are important, no? I'm tensing up. Anger level one and rising.

Then someone else steps out of the shadows and says a single, magic word: "FBI."

Bradley looks up in confusion. Swings his gun toward this new threat.

"Whoa, whoa!" says the newcomer, putting both his hands up. A badge glints.

"Don't shoot the nice federal agent," I say from the ground. "Use your head, Skip. That's what it's there for."

With great reluctance, Officer Skip Bradley lowers his gun and takes a closer look at the other man. So do I, as the agent steps into the light. He's Korean-American, in his thirties, with a face used to smiling. Amusement glints in his wide, alert eyes.

"Special Agent Ethan Jeong," he says. "Sorry to interrupt this reunion of Portsmouth PD's finest, but Ms. Allard needs to come with me."

"The fuck she does," Bradley spits at him. "You can't interfere with my arrest!"

"Actually, I can," is all Jeong says. He waits for Officer Bradley to process.

The returning protest dies in Bradley's mouth. His mental wheels may be slow to turn, but they're turning now. He knows as well as I do that the FBI has a resident agency office right here in town. Jeong will have colleagues and a supervisor to back him up. And when it comes to local blue versus the feds, the feds always win.

"Fuck," Bradley says. He doesn't stop Jeong as the agent helps me to my feet. But he does say, "Aren't you at least going to give me an explanation I can take back to the chief? He's going to piss bullets over this."

"Let him," Jeong says. "Your supervisor and my supervisor can work things out." He flings a business card at Bradley. The card flutters to the grass a few feet shy of its target.

Bradley mutters something about swinging dicks and traitor bitches as he bends to retrieve the card. At this time Jeong is walking me quickly back towards his car, parked just in front of mine.

"So is this an arrest too?" I ask.

Jeong smiles and shakes his head. "You don't see me forcing you to do anything, do you? You can walk away if you want to. But I think you're smarter than that. Sorry, I *know* you're smarter than that—I've read your file. We've passed it around the office."

I am grateful, but my gratitude reaches only so far. "What do you want from me?" I ask.

"Your help," Jeong says. "A partnership. Come on back with me to the office and my supervisor will explain everything."

I insist on another, closer look at Agent Jeong's badge, and he hands it over. It looks legit. Right now I can't imagine what kind of interest a federal agency would have in one dead white kid. But I'm curious to find out. I hop in the agent's car, and he drives us away.

So, the night is getting weirder. And colder. I wrap my jacket tighter around myself as I step out of the car. We're not far from the Piscataqua here on Daniel Street.

My situation started to feel unreal as soon as Agent Jeong intervened to save me from arrest. Now I'm not sure what to expect as he leads me into the looming hulk on Daniel Street, the McIntyre Building. I can't recall having ever gone into the big government building before, whether for business or pleasure.

Given this sense of unreality, I'm thinking anything is now possible. In short, I'm thinking a little like you.

I'm imagining that we walk into a snow-covered cathedral with a host of elves in pointy shoes greeting us to the Land of Winter's Eve. I'm picturing a burning cavern with a choir of demons in fiery balconies, singing as the Devil himself administers me the rites of damnation at an altar of virgin's blood. Surely I won't step into—an office building.

I step into an office building. It's dark and dull in the lobby, not any more exciting than the adjoining post office. And yet, and yet, I'm braced for anything to pop out on this evening of the unforeseen.

"Just up these stairs a couple of floors," says Agent Jeong lightly, leading the way. He sounds pleased, almost flirtatious, as he goes on: "You're gonna love it. The dreariest little corner of bureaucracy on the Seacoast, but what we get up to is *extremely* interesting."

"Can't wait to hear all about it," I mutter.

We walk into a forest of cubicles on the third floor. Ethan Jeong has prepared me accurately. It is dreary in here. Dark, and desperately in need of a dusting. But the tables are groaning with important-looking documents, the grey fabric walls of the cubicles are plastered with dim photographs and drawings, and the whiteboards are streaked with impossible-to-decipher diagrams. All in all, a far more mysterious air hangs over the office than I would have expected.

I thought I understood the typical investigations of the Portsmouth resident agency: fraud, corruption, online scams, kiddie porn, etc. Just like the other nine resident agencies in this region that answer to the Boston FBI field office. But I never actually worked with the local agents or even met them. My job as a patrol officer didn't call for it. Most people living around here don't even know the FBI has a Portsmouth outpost, and that's the way a spook office likes it.

Another agent, a tall Hispanic woman with a somber expression, gets up from her cubicle as soon as we come into view. "Jeong," she says. "I'll get SSA Marsters right away."

"You're a peach, Ramirez!" he sings out. Is he flirting with her, too, or is all this sunniness just standard-issue Jeong? During college, I gave up on reading men as a waste of time.

A stocky woman with iron-grey hair appears, file in hand. I sense the change in Agent Jeong's demeanor immediately upon seeing her. He's still smiling, but his body language is stiff. He stops playing with his hair. And he waits for Marsters to speak first.

Supervisory Special Agent Marsters ignores him and walks right over to me. She stands a little closer than I'm comfortable with. But I don't want to show any weakness by stepping back. Instead I meet and hold her gaze.

"You don't look like an Allard," the woman says.

Here it is. The anger churns deep in me, like volcanic activity.

SSA Marsters rubs her chin. I notice a few small hairs on it. I am hyperfocused on the agent as she goes on: "You look like a Patel to us. Or a Chatterjee. Maybe a Bannerjee. What kind of a Hindu name is 'Allard?'"

I picture slamming the SSA against the nearest cubicle wall, then forcing her head back and plucking out each one of those tiny chin hairs. Maybe one of them will turn out to be really long, and I'll just *keep pulling.* After I'm done with the chin hairs, I'll start with the hair on her head. One hank of it at a time. Once she's bald, I'll gather her hair into a pile on the desk and set it on fire. Then I'll make her eat it while it's still burning.

Trigger. I can't control the trigger. And I can't control the emotion that reacts to it. But I can control the behavior that results.

"Funny story," I say through a smile full of teeth. "Allard is my adoptive name. I grew up with adoptive parents in Manchester. As it turns out, 'Allard' is a common name in the French-Canadian community. Thank you for your interest in my family background, Agent Marsters."

Marsters stands there for another couple of beats, assessing me. And then she backs up, gives me a little more space. "Divya Benazir Allard," she finally says. "Your father's name is Jean-Paul Allard. Twenty-eight years in the Manchester PD. Your mother is Joy Allard, née Cahill. West High biology teacher, recently retired. They still live in the duplex on Varney Street that you grew up in."

My anger is fading now, as hard to hold onto as an afternoon dream. "If you've already seen my biopic," I say, "why bother with the pretense?"

Her eyes are small and mean, but full of cold intelligence. "We needed to assess your emotional maturity, Officer Allard. We're given to understand that you've had an issue with your anger in the past."

My jaw tightens. I try to contain my amusement at calling a string of smashed possessions, a full deck of ruined friendships and partnerships, an arrest, and a wrecked career an *anger issue.* Understatement of the millennium. And what's with the royal "we"?

"But your ongoing sessions with . . ." Marsters pauses, leafs through the file she's holding at her leisure, and then finally continues: ". . . Kathryn Bergman have clearly taught you a few helpful techniques. Laudable. We might only suggest to leave off the sarcastic touch at the end, Allard. Sarcasm still has its roots in anger."

"What, I'm not supposed to thank people for their endearing curiosity about my ethnicity?" I say.

The woman doesn't smile. "If we don't master our emotions, Officer Allard, our emotions master us."

I don't quibble over her persistence in calling me "Officer." It's better than "Detective," I suppose. "Is it all right if I ask why brought me here you did, Master Yoda? Or do you have any further wisdom to share first?"

Marsters snaps her file shut. She glances at Jeong before speaking again. "Has Special Agent Jeong mentioned anything about what we do here?"

I shrug. "Not really. He's been a good dog, if that's what you're asking."

"This RA differs from the others under Boston's jurisdiction in one key regard," Marsters says. "Are you familiar, Allard, with the past initiative of the United States government known as Project Stargate?"

I find that staring into those cold eyes has worn me out. I picture a tall drink, an escape. But I also have my pride, and my curiosity. Soon, hopefully, this will all be over. "I don't know. Might've read about it at some point. Is that when the CIA was trying to give American soldiers the power of ESP? To spy on the Russians from afar, or something?"

Marsters gives me a half-nod. "That was only the barest beginning of the experiments that fell under the umbrella of Stargate. The operation code-named GRILL FLAME gave the CIA remote viewing into the hostage situation in Tehran. And the FBI got a large piece of the Stargate pie to explore domestic applications for what might be termed paranormal or parapsychological abilities."

"Mmkay." *This* is what these folks get up to when they don't have an extortioner to bust? And to think I'd felt silly daydreaming about elves and devils.

"What's most germane here is—based on decades of intense and highly classified research, the FBI assigned extra responsibilities and resources to resident agencies in certain geographic locations. Locations with . . . strategic potential, as determined by what you might call para-data miners. Most of the locations never panned out. Glitches in the data, evidence turned to phantoms, or simple human error. However—Portsmouth never dropped off that map."

Strategic potential? I have no idea what she's talking about, but I nod too. "Portsmouth's a real special place."

"You have no conception of just how special," Marsters says. She clears her throat—apparently she's not going to tell me about all that special stuff at this early point in our relationship. "We have an interest in finding out just what happened to that boy. Tsoukalas. The Portsmouth police are not inclined to be helpful in this matter. Quite the opposite, for reasons unknown to us. You, however, will be helpful. And you'll tell us everything you know."

"Will I?" I say. "That doesn't sound like me. A little too generous."

"Here is the bargain we propose," the SSA goes on, as if I haven't spoken. Clearly she's sick of my shit already. "You proceed with your informal investigation. You feed all of your findings to us, via Special Agent Jeong. In return, we will use our considerable power to clear your way. We'll keep your old colleagues off your back. And . . . we will tell you everything we know about the murder of Hannah Ryder."

I suspected they would use you as a bargaining chip. But it still hits me in the stomach when she says it. It's the first time—if you don't count the not-so-sly allusion by Anonymous Caller—that I've heard someone outside my own head call your death a murder. Not an accident, and not a fucking suicide. A murder.

I think back to the Portsmouth PD patronizing me,

putting me off, my old boss Chief Akerman cutting me loose just when my questions got too uncomfortable. "Not inclined to be helpful," indeed. Maybe SSA Marsters is just talking out of her ass and manipulating me, but my anger takes the bait. I fume at the cops who'd dared pretend to be my friends. And the *Portsmouth Porthole,* eagerly dismissing me as a goddamn loon.

I'm trembling. I need to smash something.

Instead, I close my eyes, and then I open them again and I say to Marsters in a perfectly even tone: "Why don't you investigate Tsoukalas's death yourself?"

In the dimness of the office, it's hard to read the supervisory special agent's face. "We may be located here, but—we are not part of this community. You are. Even if you feel like an exile, you still have far greater access in Portsmouth than we do. Our specialty is . . . force. Yours must be persuasion."

So she basically thinks I'm a detective after all. I appreciate the vote of confidence. But I'll have to stretch myself to fit the role I never got the chance to earn.

"Do we have a deal, Allard?" Marsters adds sharply. "Our time is short."

I'd be an idiot to refuse this offer, as long as I'm already determined to wade into ethical murk in my pursuit of the truth. But something about this whole arrangement makes my skin crawl. Why would the FBI care so much about a dead community college kid? What's their stake?

I sigh, run my hand through my hair, and decide that their motivation is not my problem. My self-appointed duty is simply the following: to find out why two wrist-implanting fitness nuts met their respective ends.

"Fine," I say. "But I hope you don't mean to have Agent Jeong babysit me the whole time. I don't deal well with babysitters."

"I'll just check in with you from time to time," says Jeong. He's got an easy grin. "You can stay up as late as you want, and even watch scary movies. Best babysitter ever, right?"

Marsters turns from me without acknowledging our bargain and walks away. I guess that's all I'm going to get. Ethan Jeong smirks at me. "How about I escort you out, Divya?"

And so ends my brief visit to the FBI resident agency on Daniel Street. The moon is out, though clouds keep scudding across it. Jeong parts from me in the parking lot with just a few words: "We'll be in touch."

I notice that my car is now in the lot. The keys are on the front seat. One of the other SAs must have pulled re-parking duty. I get in and adjust the seat to my liking.

It's late. I'm no longer thinking clearly, as I'm just not used to the second shift anymore. I've gotten soft working security for the nine-to-fivers. I should probably put my adventures to bed and start fresh tomorrow.

But—I'm worried about Akerman's cleanup crew lapping me while I sleep. Right now I have a significant advantage over them: the DVD.

I need to get to Graham's pair of lovers before the police do.

5

F or the first time, I think about how my actions tonight could affect my day job.

It's a fleeting thought, but it leaves me rattled. After I cursed out Chief Akerman, and subsequently the entire Portsmouth Police Department, he fired me. He may have had no other option, but at the time I just took it as further evidence of his corruption. I spent months prying where I shouldn't have pried, scrabbling for scraps of information and alienating my friends and former colleagues, telling anyone who would listen that the department was rotten to the core. Either they didn't care what happened to you—or they were covering up the truth!

My hobbies during that period included raging at the TV and getting shitfaced, sometimes simultaneously. I shunned the attractions that made tourists cream themselves over Portsmouth, turning away from the waterfront charms of Prescott Park and the isle of New Castle. I preferred to drown myself at State Street Saloon, or the Portsmouth Book and Bar if I was feeling a little fancier.

I only broke the cycle once I started actually listening to

my court-mandated therapist, Kathryn Bergman. (You would like her, I think.) By that time, I was down to pocket change for my savings. If I could no longer pay even the cheap rent of my apartment, I'd end up on the street. Pretty much nobody in town wanted to hire me, not with my reputation. My parents kept urging me to move back to Manchester, move in with them. But that felt like it would be the final nail in my already decaying ambition.

Then someone took a chance on me. Jacobi Investment Advisors actually responded to my resume when I applied for a security opening in their relatively new offices downtown. Mr. Baldini, the head of security, was willing to hear me out. It turns out I had helped a friend of his while I was on the force. Mr. Baldini was a recovering alcoholic, and he'd learned the value of forgiveness.

I've been a loyal employee of JIA for the months since. Now, if I do anything to embarrass them, I'll be letting down not just the company (which I care little for), but also Mr. Baldini (whom I do care very much about).

So I resolve, now, to be more careful than I've been so far. It's not just my battered reputation on the line. What do they say, no man is an island? All islands are connected to the earth, somewhere under the water. Even New Castle's got bridges to the mainland.

It's too late at night to look for Wallace and Neria at Great Bay Community College. Most likely, they're home at their apartment off Islington Street. But I find myself driving past their street and pulling into the Hannaford shopping plaza.

I know! Technically I'm still legally barred from going anywhere near the Tenacious Trainers gym. And I don't know what I expect to find there. I've been down this road before. But the problem then was that I tried to break into the place. I skipped the persuasion step completely. If I could just talk to someone—nicely, politely . . .

It's supposed to be a 24-hour gym. But the front door's locked. There are no windows to peer inside. Knocking yields no response.

And then I pick up on a coppery smell.

Maybe others would miss it. It's faint. But I smelled blood many times during my short career as a police officer, and there's no mistaking it now. Where is it coming from?

The gym is an end unit in the plaza; I walk around to the back. The smell gets stronger. I see a dumpster in the back of the place—and a pool of blood on the pavement. Hmm.

I check for my gun, and then remember that it's not there. I only get to carry while I'm working at JIA. I whirl, looking for assailants. That blood is fresh. I see no one in the darkness.

Having assured myself that I won't get jumped, I open up the dumpster. The only trash inside this dumpster is a corpse.

I scramble away and the lid slams down. I fumble for my flashlight. Then I summon the will to open the lid again and shine the light down on the mound of stinking flesh inside.

The face is unmistakable, battered though it is. I've seen that face earlier tonight in photos (and, memorably, in a video). It's Graham Tsoukalas.

What the fuck?

Graham Tsoukalas is supposed to be dead on Peirce Island, not in a dumpster behind the Tenacious Trainers gym.

How did the cops fuck up the body ID on the island?

Okay. I've found a body; I should call it in to the Portsmouth PD. But—I'm haunted by Christine Figueroa's warning. Akerman showed up at the *Porthole* office to clam them up about this case. Just like with you. No, the *last* thing I should do is surrender custody of this body to the likely compromised police force.

I sigh and hoist myself into the dumpster to take a closer look at the body. Graham's face has taken a noticeable beating. His neck is twisted at an unnatural angle, which I don't think was caused by being deposited into a dumpster. Then again, I'm not a pathologist.

Unremarkable clothes: jeans, sweater, a barn jacket, unlaced hiking boots on his feet. Wait. I push up his jacket and sweater sleeves. I want to get a good look at this "gadget." I never got the chance to examine yours.

Both of Graham's wrists are unblemished and unimplanted. No sign of a biometric device in either one—nor any sign of such a device having been *removed.* No scars, no stitches.

"Fuck," I whisper. Anonymous Caller manipulated me. He made me think Graham had a link to you, just so I'd investigate his friend's death.

But . . . No. Milly and Ulrich saw a gadget in Graham's wrist. Ulrich was the one to *call* it a "gadget." And Mrs. Tsoukalas confirmed that Graham had the implant. It's disappeared. Someone took it. Somehow. Though it'd take someone with expert surgical skills to leave the skin this smooth and seemingly unbroken.

That sound right to you?

I ignore the impossibility of this detail. I'll have to come back to it. What else? I check his pockets and they're empty. His fingernails are clean, no sign of dirt. In fact, except for that nasty beating and neck wound, Graham looks pretty spanking spotless. No stab wounds, nothing that would bleed much.

So whose blood is on the ground?

I climb out, slam the lid down, and ponder what to do next. Graham isn't supposed to be *here*. Who moved his fucking body, and *how*? Akerman couldn't be this slimy, could he?

As I walk back to the lot, I put in a quick call to Agent Jeong. I've promised to keep the FBI in the loop, after all. But I don't have to show them my *whole* hand, do I? I'd rather keep them one step behind. I would hate to see Marsters bigfoot me just as I'm closing in on the truth.

"Yes?" Jeong says.

"Found a body," I say. "In the dumpster behind the Tenacious Trainers gym, in the Islington plaza. You'll want to see it. And you'll want to secure it too, before the Portsmouth PD comes sniffing around."

"Another body? Wait, who—"

I hang up. Feeling like a jerk, but I need to keep the lead.

6

U nlike me, you grew up in Portsmouth. You had a genuine local pride, too. Despite all that false gods talk, you loved to hang out in the shops and restaurants downtown, and you loved to watch the people go by. The people you knew. You made me feel like a local, too. I always appreciated that. I loved to see this city through your eyes.

Wallace Riggs and Neria Francoeur live together in an apartment building in a neighborhood not far from where you used to live. That's why I'm thinking of you when I arrive. It's just off Islington Street, not far from the plaza where I just found Graham Tsoukalas's body. It's not anywhere near the water, not a target for luxury condo development yet (though they are creeping westward), but I'm sure the rents are still jacked up way beyond what they ought to be.

I've pulled up a distance away, like before at the Tsoukalas household, so as not to announce myself. Now that I'm not a cop anymore, I have the luxury of being a sneak. I approach the house quietly and cautiously. Wallace and Neria live on the bottom floor of this four-story house. I can see lights on; I know they're home.

Graham called his DVD "Backup." Was he blackmailing his friends? Hmm. Could be a motive.

I creep to the side of the house, to peer through the windows and see what I'm in for. I wish I had a gun, just in case. But I can't carry around the one I use for my security job. I'm on high alert because these kids could be responsible for making not just one but two people into corpses.

The lights wink out. The plan I've cooked up in my head dissipates when the front door of the house opens. The two college students come out clutching backpacks. It's hard to see many other details in the dark. They've got their heads close together, and I can't pick up what they're saying, but they definitely sound distressed.

I recalibrate my plan. I don't have the authority to arrest them or stop them in any way. If I call in Jeong and company for backup, these kids will be gone by the time the agents arrive.

My best bet is to follow them. There's value in seeing where they end up. I hope they aren't going far, though, because I'm pretty damned tired.

They haven't noticed me yet, so I take a step sideways into the nearest driveway and conceal myself behind a porch. I watch them as they throw their backpacks into a red sedan parked on the street. As they get in the car, I sneak back over to my own ride. I start it up and follow them at a discreet distance.

Their sedan heads not for I-95 and the wider world, as I expect, but instead down Islington back toward the downtown. Intrigued, I follow. Having killed two people, are Wallace and Neria now going to grab a late-night coffee at Breaking New Grounds, or what?

They don't stop for coffee. They drive to Marcy Street and park the car.

They then get out, curiously bringing only one of the backpacks, and the two college students head into Prescott Park.

The police are still set up at the bridge area. Now the TV news crews have arrived, or at least the first couple of vans. It's becoming a carnival, flashing lights chasing the darkness from the waterfront.

I've managed to find a spot not far away from where Wallace and Neria parked. A small miracle bestowed by the parking gods of Portsmouth. I follow the students, now more confused than ever. In my experience, criminals usually *don't* return to the scene of the crime. Their concern is to get the fuck away and stay away.

Wallace and Neria cross through the formal garden with its bubbling fountains. I track them among the pink flowering crabapples, passing the beds of coleus and creeping zinnia and fuschia. On the other side, the couple heads east—rather than southeast toward the bridge to Peirce Island. Instead, their destination is the wharves, where a three-hundred-year-old warehouse overlooks the water. They're in a hurry. I'm not; I'm just a petite brown woman out for a nighttime stroll in a public park.

They open the door to the warehouse. Funny, I assumed the building would be locked. After a long career of storing fish and grains, the Sheafe Warehouse functions nowadays as an art gallery. I consider calling Agent Jeong—I'm not confident that I can corner both of them in the warehouse. I recall there's a door on the river side, too, offering another exit.

But I leave my phone in my pocket. I don't want anyone

denying me the chance to squeeze Graham's friends for information.

I open the warehouse door a crack. I peer inside.

The kids have their backs to me. Artwork lines the walls on either side. In the wall facing the river, rather than a door, there's a large, fiery *hole*. A hole with darkness inside.

I shake my head—I simply don't know what I'm looking at. Some kind of trick mirror? A modern-art display with a video screen?

When I view it at a different angle, moving my head, it doesn't seem *to* move. I've got a strange, cold feeling in my stomach. Marsters's words swim back into my head: *Portsmouth is a special place for reasons you can't even imagine.*

The guy, Wallace, is digging in his backpack. Neria is leaning over him anxiously, while stealing occasional glances at the burning hole-*thing*. With them both distracted, now is the perfect time to announce myself. I've decided by now that I don't give a shit about what I have the "authority" to do. I'm just going to do it.

I creep up to them. Just as the wooden boards creak under my feet and betray me, I grab the girl by the arm. "Stay where you are!"

Neria jerks in my grip. But I've got a good hold on her with both hands. Wallace stumbles upright, fumbling, and a plastic Hannaford bag drops out of his hands to the floor. He's holding onto his backpack, though. He looks at me with wide, scared, angry eyes. "Let her—"

"*Run!*" Neria screams at him.

Wallace hesitates. He's a big guy. He could try to over-power me through sheer mass. Or at least knock me away from his girlfriend. But he's torn. His eyes rove the ware-house. He's looking for my backup.

"I'm not here to hurt you," I growl, "but I need to talk to

you about Graham Tsoukalas. And *that*. Stop struggling, kid."

Again, Neria screams at Wallace to run. This time he takes her suggestion and bolts. I almost let Neria go and chase him, just because I fucking hate to see someone get away. But this bird's in my hand.

She still makes a valiant effort to get away, twisting in my grip and clawing at my face. I treasure both of my eyes, so I use my knee to slam her down and then I get on top of her. She's a skinny thing. I can manage this.

"Ugh," she says against the boards. "Are you going to arrest me?"

"I'm not a cop," I say. Surprising how it still stings to say. "But I *am* investigating Graham Tsoukalas's death. I reserve the right to turn you over to the actual police if I determine that you're a murderer and/or a pain in my ass."

Neria grunts. Presses against me in a feeble attempt to get me off her. At the physical contact, I have a sudden, unwelcome mental picture of Neria in the video, getting double-teamed by Wallace and Graham. Willing participant, or coerced into it? What kind of woman is this?

I'd better make my fact-finding quick. Milly, Ulrich, and who knows however many other Portsmouth cops are within spitting distance. Not to mention the rest of the media camped out at the bridge. Anyone outside might have heard Neria's screams.

"Why are you investigating this if you're not with the police?" she says, lifting her head.

"I'm doing this for Graham's parents," I say. A half-truth. Mrs. Tsoukalas *did* give me her blessing.

Did I just hear one of the cops calling out? Is someone coming in this direction? I'll take to take Neria and relocate, much as I hate to leave behind this . . . burning hole thing.

I poke her between the shoulder blades. "I'll let you up, but you have to promise not to attack me or try to run."

"I promise," Neria says.

Right. The faults in this plan are obvious, but I haven't left myself with any choice. I should have called Jeong. Reluctantly I ease off the girl, keeping a careful eye on her. Neria climbs to her feet and dusts herself off.

"Who's the body on the island?" I ask.

Neria stares at me. She has pretty, shimmering dark eyes. "What?"

"The body the police found," I say. "It sure as hell isn't Graham, so who is it?"

"It *is* Graham," she says.

"Don't give me that . . ." I say, but I check myself. I'm out of time. Ulrich, or Akerman, finding me here with a hostage would be a disaster. Clearly we'll have to explore Neria's mistaken belief in further detail elsewhere.

But before we leave the warehouse, I *have* to ask her one other thing. I jab my finger at the burning hole. "What the fuck is that thing? Some kind of slideshow projection?" I try to lead her closer so I can inspect it further, but Neria stiffens and resists me.

"*Don't go near it,*" she says.

I try forcing her forward again, but she fights me. Then a siren whoops, and we both jump. It sounds like it's right outside. It's not—just a distortion bouncing off the river—but Neria takes advantage of my grip loosening and breaks away from me.

She's off. Gone. Before I can contemplate leaving this floating, burning hole behind.

I know I could catch up with her if I pushed myself. But the projection, or whatever it is, has mesmerized me. Just now I think I hear a sound coming from the hole, a kind of high whistling like wind. It's not real—openings don't just appear in the middle of the air—but it fascinates me.

Approaching it, I trip over something. It's the plastic grocery store bag that Wallace dropped. Inside are several large pieces of . . . coal. Odd. Someone's getting screwed by Santa this Christmas, but it's only May. What would the kid need coal for?

I leave the bag of coal and walk around the hole. Behind it, I do see the door to the river, giving a view of the shipyard lights across the water. The burning hole looks the same to me from every angle, which should be impossible. I've never seen any kind of art display that involves a fucking 3D hologram, or whatever. It's uncanny. Wrong.

You'd be even more fascinated by this thing than I am now.

Neria warned me to stay from the hole. But she might be a murderer, and I need a closer look. I put my face up next to it. Looking. Listening.

It's *not* darkness inside. There's—another place. A place that isn't Portsmouth.

I catch a glimpse of stone. Stone surface. An altar? The flicker of some fire deep inside, different from the burning fire surrounding this hole. I don't feel any heat on my face from the fire bordering the hole. It's like that part's a trick. But I do feel, and hear, wind whistling from the place within the hole.

"A Little Bit Enormous," indeed. Portsmouth stretches in directions I hadn't imagined. Would Councilor Stone approve?

I shouldn't do this. I shouldn't. But it strikes me that this, uh, phenomenon—this otherworldly shit happening right in front of me—could factor into my case after all.

Maybe it's a self-destructive urge that propels me

forward, the same urge that Kathryn tried to help me quell over all these long months. In taking a step forward, I'm really taking a step back. To the old, mad Allard. But in this moment, I don't fucking care.

In this moment, I pretend I'm you. Flying free and without a goddamn worry in the world. Everything an adventure.

I step through the hole, the door, with you in my heart.

7

Sensations tug at me as I go through. Not burning, thank God, but tingling. In the back of my brain. In the pit of my stomach. In my fingertips. Between my legs. For a moment my mind tumbles into pure sensory reaction.

Then I remember to breathe. And I'm standing in a faded grey stone chamber with a ceiling that comes together in a point. Like I'm standing inside a pyramid. A pyramidal temple? There *is* an altar in the center of the chamber, made of the same pitted grey stones as the walls of the temple, topped by a grotesque, ten-foot-tall dark creature that I'm really hoping is just a statue. Glowing yellow stones are set into the walls between the grey bricks at regular intervals, the only source of light here.

I command my hands to stop shaking, but it's no use. I'm going to be in half-seizure mode until I can wrap my tiny little mind around what the fuck just happened, and what is happening now. Where I *am* now.

I turn to take a look behind me. Where I've come from.

Thankfully, I see a burning hole on *this* side of the universe, revealing a distorted view of the interior of the Sheafe Warehouse. Here, the hole isn't floating; it's set into a wall, in the center of a vast and intricate mosaic depicting several pairs of fanciful flying beasts that resemble serpents or dragons, twisting around each other in combat or maybe embrace.

I can go back. I'm not trapped here. With that thought, I'm able to take a few more breaths, and get my shaking under limited control (still would be a pretty shit typer on a smartphone right now, though).

"Okay," I say aloud. "Welcome to Planet What-the-Hell."

Population: Allard, and who else?

The sound of my own voice fails to comfort me, though it's the only familiar element here. My legs are trembly as I walk forward. The altar seems like a logical first stop. I wait for the triangular black thing to show a hint of movement, but it remains still. I circle around it and examine the glossy surface of the statue: if I had to guess, I'd say obsidian. Same material that constitutes the darkest parts of the mosaic on the wall, in fact.

The statue depicts a: hmm: the only thing I can think is "giant slug." Nasty fricking creepy-crawly rendered in as loving detail as the mosaic. Why? Clearly a master artisan created these works, but who? And *why*? The giant slug hardly has what could be termed a face, yet it seems to be looking at me regardless of my viewing angle. I shiver, look down, and notice a far more mundane object at its base.

My first crazy thought is it's a welcome guide and a map. Or a feedback form (Would I recommend this venue for conferences, yes or no?).

Instead, what lies on the rough grey surface of the altar is a small sketchpad. It's not from around here, I'm guessing.

I pick up the sketchpad. It opens to a drawing resembling the flying-beast mosaic behind me. I flip to a drawing of the giant slug statue. Someone from my world came here as a tourist before I did.

Graham?

It looks like there are other drawings and notes as well. I tuck the sketchpad into my jacket pocket. I'd rather leaf through it at a later time, when I'm not in a strange alien temple.

I touch the strange glowing yellow stones set into the wall. They feel warm. I'm completely baffled about what *these* are made of.

The sound of whistling wind registers in my ears. Sounds like a hell of a storm outside. What's outside? Unfortunately, there are no windows in this chamber, but there is a doorway on the far end. The doorway is oddly vaulted into a triangular shape, just like the shape of the temple itself (and the rough shape of the giant slug). I pluck up my courage and go through the doorway.

Now I find myself in another stone room. The sloped ceiling is lower and the room is broader. The sound of the wind is much louder in here. A set of huge, shiny black (more obsidian?) doors form yet another triangle in the front of this foyer, if that's what the room is. And now, yes, there are glassless windows, eight or nine on both my left and right. They're looking out onto—what I can only mentally process as a hellscape.

Much as I'd care not to, I approach the nearest window, feeling the wind whip my face. I need to have a closer look ... to know if this is *real* or not.

The window shows me a view of a blasted, barren landscape under a sky too full of stars. When I say too full, I mean that there is a seemingly impossible depth of white light up there, more than I've ever seen on Earth. The brutal wind washes over the land, scrubbing it of vegetation. But there are things out there definitely *enjoying* the wind—playing in it. Rolling in the gusts, in the air. In tangled pairs. They let out terrifying crackling screeches, full of hard consonants that almost sound like language.

Flying beasts. Horrible dark scaled flying twinned and twining beasts. They look much like the creatures rendered in the mosaic.

Some of them soar and dart off in the distance. Some of them are—much closer. Bigger in my field of view. I think one pair of them has just noticed my face in the window.

I whisper a curse to myself and backpedal. I stumble away from the window, into the center of the temple foyer. It looks like the winged beasts are coming closer to this place. But I find I can't move my legs anymore.

Fuck. Run!

What breaks my paralysis is a quick glance over at the other wall of the place. I see oily yellowed eyes peeking in through *those* windows: another pair of flying beasts has arrived. They're even closer, now, just outside the temple, seizing the window frames with their claws and breathing foul miasmas into the space. Maybe they all smelled me. That's four of the long, twined serpents with their hooked claws and their rows and rows of katana-sized teeth.

Their hard, crackling shrieks—no, *exclamations*—box my ears.

Terror frees my legs to run. I go back through the triangular doorway. I don't dare look behind me. I have only one destination, and it's the burning hole framed by the mosaic.

I make it there without either of the monsters eating me from behind. And I close my eyes as I enter the hole. I feel that same tingling as before as I pass through, spreading throughout my body. This time it doesn't feel as bad. Or maybe I'm just getting used to it.

I step out onto the solid floorboards of the old warehouse in Prescott Park in Portsmouth in New Hampshire in the United States of Planet Earth.

I breathe a huge sigh of relief. In the clear. No more other world, no more incomprehensible horrors to contend with.

Until I remember that the burning hole behind me *is still open.* Has been open this whole time. It's too small for any one of those flying beasts to fit through—but just one of those hooked claws would fit, and that'd be enough to kill me.

Please let this be over. I take a few trembling steps away from the hole and then feel brave enough to whirl around to face the sight of where I've just come from. I need to see if any of the beasts has torn down the grey stones of the temple to chase me. Could they rip the burning hole wider? If they destroy the temple's mosaic wall on the other side, what happens here?

I catch a glimpse of dark skin. A shadowed *someone* is standing right in front of me. That's when the fist hits me, full in the face, and I go down. Blackness descends.

WHEN I WAKE UP, I'm lying on the floor with a tremendous headache. It's still nighttime. I'm still near the burning hole. But now I'm completely naked. Agent Ethan Jeong crouches over me.

"Allard?"

He must have slapped my face just before I came to. My cheeks are ringing almost as much as my skull. I nod wearily at him. "Ugh. Beast of a night. Would you mind not staring at my tits?"

Jeong coughs and struggles to meet my gaze. Failing to do so, he stares at the floor. "You okay?" he hisses. "What the hell's going on?"

"I . . . have no idea," I admit. I'm not mentally ready to talk about the things I just saw in the—other place. "How did you get here?"

"Been continuing to follow you. Marsters is yearning for updates. Do you want my coat?"

"Please."

Jeong takes off his coat and drops it on the floor without looking at me. I put it on and stand up. It almost does the job, because he's taller and broader than me. But the bottom of my ass is still hanging out, and anyone who wants a look at my bush doesn't have to dip their head very far. This will not do. Also, I'm still cold.

"Did Riggs and Francoeur do this to you?" he asks.

I shake my head. "No. I mean, I don't think so. I don't know. Somebody got me from behind. But it wasn't somebody as tall as Wallace Riggs. And Neria had run off—and she was afraid of the hole, so she wouldn't have gotten that close to it."

"The hole," Ethan Jeong says. Now he's contemplating that gateway to nightmares. He tilts his head just as I did, trying to see it from a different angle. "That's . . . not good."

He isn't as surprised as I'd expect him to be, looking at a portal to another dimension. He just looks worried. Bells of suspicion clang in my battered head. *Operation Stargate. Project GRILL FLAME.* What do he and Marsters know?

"Do you know how to close that hole?" he says.

"Do *I* know . . .?" I give him a frustrated look. "No, Agent Jeong, I do not. And I suggest your people cordon off the whole area around this thing until you do figure out how to close it."

Jeong nods. "Right. I'll make some calls in just a minute. For now, let's get out of here."

Jeong and I exit the warehouse and hurry through Prescott Park. I'm still confused as to why my attacker would need my clothes. It's not like they were designer. He or she could have just taken my wallet if they wanted my money and/or ID.

We're lucky enough not to run into any cops or media on our way to Jeong's car. I can just picture the reactions from my old colleagues, seeing me like this. We drive over to Pleasant Street, and that's when I realize the thief made off with my apartment keys as well.

"Okay, give me a minute or two," I say. I spring out of the car, still wearing Jeong's coat, and apply pressure to the foyer door. I'm in luck: someone has once again forgotten to close the door all the way. Not me—I always check—but probably someone who works for the small nonprofit occupying the floor below my apartment. It's the first time I'm glad for the shoddy security here. I pound up the dark stairs to the landing outside my apartment door.

No such luck with this door. Divya Allard's home is her castle. I hesitate only briefly before grabbing a hammer that my landlord carelessly left on the landing, and I go to town on the glass window in the old door. It's oddly satisfying to smash the thing, even though I know this will be coming out of my deposit. Then again, given the trail of inanimate objects that I've ruthlessly murdered since you died—a cell phone, three coffee mugs, two plates, various mirrors, even a printer on one memorable occasion—I suppose I shouldn't be surprised.

Once I've pounded through the chickenwire underneath the glass, too, I reach through and open my own door. I wriggle into new underwear, pants, and a long-sleeved shirt, and grab my backup pair of shoes. Then I return to Jeong, closing the foyer door firmly behind me on the way. I'll deal with how to re-enter the building later.

"You made quite the racket," he says. "Ever consider leaving a spare set of keys under one of those fake rocks?"

"Sure, that wouldn't look suspicious in an indoor hallway."

"So now what?" he says. "I've got Agents Barnes and McGuinness maintaining a perimeter around the hole. They're reliable, but they'll be looking to us for initiative."

"I think closing it should be the priority," I say. It hits me that Wallace and Neria might have shown up at the burning hole for that very purpose. They certainly hadn't seemed eager to go *into* the hole, so what else might they have been doing there? The hapless two no longer seem like viable murder suspects to me, if they were willing to confront such a nightmare with no apparent personal gain. "We need to find Graham's friends/lovers. They may be the only ones who know how to do the job."

Then I remember the sketchpad that I grabbed from the other side of the portal. If it had been Graham's—if Graham had been the one to *open* that hole—then maybe Graham had known how to close it too. He might have even written how to do so in that sketchpad. Pity it had disappeared with my jacket. Damn.

Oh, and that fucking DVD! God, my jacket would be quite the treasure to whoever snagged it.

"Hold on," Jeong says. The man peers into the window of a nearby bar with a big TV. The TV is playing a news report instead of the latest ballgame—and two familiar faces are on the screen. Along with the words *TSOUKALAS'S FRIENDS BEING QUESTIONED.*

"Shit," I say. "The PD's got 'em."

The agent gives me a sardonic smile. "Your pals. Your move."

8

What would you have thought about gateways to other universes or dimensions?

Would you have been freaked out—or would you have seen it as an opportunity? An opening to an array of infinite possibilities?

Given your New Age field trip to Sedona, I'm thinking the latter. Your mind was permanently hinged open. My mind, on the other hand, narrow in its focus and cautious about new information, strains to deny what I saw. I'm finding that the less I think about that other world, the better. Because I could disappear down a vortex of madness if I really dwell on the implications.

No, it's better to focus on practical matters. Like the job. And I'm going to make sure nobody ever crosses through that hole ever again. From either direction.

The Portsmouth Police Department and City Hall crouch together in a hilltop complex overlooking South Mill Pond and the downtown skyline. Though the buildings themselves are ugly and outdated, the grassy hill is a pretty spot, especially at this time of year with the pondside cherry blossom trees still showing some color.

I've been strenuously avoiding the municipal complex ever since the Horrible Time of last year. I hoped I'd never have to go there again, in fact. Even if that meant never renewing my car registration.

Which is why I'm really dragging my feet, and not resenting Agent Jeong's tagalong presence at all, as we pull into the lot on that hilltop and approach the station. This is going to be the worst.

I keep flashing back to the media crowding me in that same parking lot. Especially Kuhn of the *Portsmouth Porthole,* merciless as he sinks his fangs into the story of a lifetime.

"Officer Allard, how long were you lovers with the deceased and did your supervisors know about it?"

"Officer Allard, have your rage issues ever affected your job before now?"

"Officer Allard, tell me more about this department-wide conspiracy!"

I shudder. Jeong raises a concerned eyebrow. "Are you all right? You've been through a lot tonight, Divya. I'm sure if we come back in the morning—"

"—then Wallace and Neria will no longer be here," I finished for him. "These are leads. We chase them while they're hot. Don't worry about me, Agent Jeong. Now that I have pants back on, I'm aces."

We walk into the small wedge of lobby surrounded by bulletproof glass. Portsmouth may be the City of the Open Door, but to get any further into the PD, visitors need to be buzzed in by the station officer. And she's looking at me with extreme skepticism. *Hello, Officer Haring. Sorry I called you that name that one time.*

I see a wall of blue in the larger lobby beyond the glass. Chief Akerman himself, a wiry, fit man with a perpetually grim expression on his face, is leaning against the tall case of old police memorabilia. Never been one for the pleasures of this world, our Henry. He's therefore a perfect fit for the job, I suppose, though I always suspected he'd be happier as the chief in a city with a higher body count. Well, Portsmouth's opioid surge might just make up for it.

Akerman's expression just gets grimmer when he sees the two of us. Piotrowski, Daniels, and the other officers close ranks around him. I'm getting *plenty* of dirty looks. Though the Horrible Time is blurry now around the edges, I can still remember the personalized insults I threw at each one of them. Deserved or not.

"FBI," Jeong says to Officer Haring and flashes his badge. "Let us through."

She presses the button to unlock the door. But Akerman blocks us as soon as we walk in.

"No civilians past this area," he says, though he can't manage to meet my eyes; he's looking at Agent Jeong instead. Could be he's remembering when I jabbed my finger into his chest over and over, naming him a "hypocritical shit-smearing cover artist" and a "hat-fucking, scum-sucking bullshit artist" (which is a lot of ground for the same person to cover, I know).

Yeah, I was pretty awful. I swear, Kathryn has helped me so much since then—though just seeing Akerman again, I trigger again. Just a little. I automatically picture myself smashing open that memorabilia case and beating Akerman about the face and neck with an antique billy club.

I briefly close my eyes to recenter.

"Special circumstances," says Jeong formally, though with a smile. He flashes his FBI badge at my old boss. "Special Agent Ethan Jeong. I am working closely with Officer Allard here on a matter urgent to the state. We have a pressing need to speak to Wallace Riggs and Neria Francoeur."

"*Officer* Allard?!" Akerman says, in a rare flash of temper. "Listen to me, asshole. Skip Bradley told me how you pulled rank on him tonight at the Tsoukalas house and superseded Allard's arrest. I expect a written explanation and full justification from your SSA about *that*. And now you think you can just walk in here and boss around this entire fucking department? I'll need to speak to the God-damned director of the FBI before I let you in, do you hear me?!"

Jeong gives him an apologetic shrug and shake of the head. "I know. It sucks. We totally respect your local authority here. But I'm acting to prevent an imminent threat, and I have full power under the Constitution to do so."

"Threat? What threat?" Akerman looks both concerned and pissed off to be out of the loop.

"We have reason to believe that the deceased, Graham Tsoukalas, belonged to a terrorist group," Ethan Jeong says. *Terrorist.* In the hands of law enforcement, that's a magic word, isn't it? "And that his friends Riggs and Francoeur may be implicated in that group as well."

Akerman's lips twist into a grimace. But, interestingly, he doesn't seem as shocked as the other officers around him. For comparison, while Akerman stews and stays planted where he is, Piotrowski's mouth hangs open and his body posture has changed into a hunch. Daniels's hands are balled into fists, as if he'll go kung fu on any terrorist who'd dare set foot inside his little seaside town. The other guys look surprised, fearful, and amped up as well.

I know for many of my former colleagues, it's their secret

and most cherished dream: to take down at least one T-word before they retire. Even one without brown skin will do.

"I'm glad you brought up my boss, SSA Marsters, by the way," Jeong says. "I am acting with her authority, but you're welcome to give her a call. You've dealt with Agent Marsters before, haven't you?"

Now this seems to give Akerman pause. I silently thank Marsters for whatever she did to twist his balls in the past.

"All right," says the chief. "They're in interview rooms 1 and 2. Tell Officer Fragonard and Detective Ulrich you have my blessing to proceed. But God damn you both, if there's even a whiff of lies about this, I'll sue the entire FBI and throw you both in jail. And I'll see that Allard, at least, never comes back out."

As he opens one of the secure doors for us, he mumbles the words "crazy bitch" under his breath, taking a page from Bradley's phrasebook.

I'll admit. Sometimes your constant rebellion against authority struck me as a kind of self-caricature. Sometimes I wanted to shake you by the shoulders and say: *Really? Are you ready to defend* yourself *against the guy who'd slit your throat to pay for his next fentanyl?*

But you never disrespected or disparaged *me* as a police officer. Certainly I never heard you say a word in my presence about how cops are "pigs" or smelling bacon. You recognized that, for me, upholding the law was my calling, and that I did a damn good job of it, too. That's probably why I think of you as I walk through the long institutional corridors of the police station, the corridors I thought I'd never walk again. For every moment I worked here, I always had your support.

I do wonder what you would think of me now. Bending and twisting the rules in my own search for the truth.

Would you be proud of me for acting just a little more like you? Or would you condemn me for betraying my own principles?

Guess I'll never know.

The station used to be a hospital, and the place still has the same antiseptic charm. We pass the animal control office and the roll call room, and we enter the cubicle cluster where the detectives work. Officer Milly Fragonard and Detective Ben Ulrich are standing outside interview room 1, as promised. Room 2 is farther down the wall. Milly looks dismayed when she sees me; Ulrich just gives me an intrigued smile, as if he's expecting the buildup to a good joke.

"Well, the other Injun returns," he says. "And this time she's got a new friend. Whom do I have the pleasure?"

I watch Jeong size up the other man. The agent does not look impressed. "Agent Jeong, FBI. We have Chief Akerman's authority to interrogate your detainees immediately. Sound good to you?"

"Mmm," says Ulrich. He doesn't move. "I just softened each of them up. They need just a few more minutes to stew and then they'll lay themselves out on a plate. I'd *prefer* to be the one to finish this, if you don't mind. I'm the one who first spoke to the reporting officer. I was the first detective on the scene. I'm not about to hand this over to the FBI, you feel me?"

"Stand the fuck aside," I say. I thought I was keeping my irritation and anger in check. But *fuck* is a trigger in itself, and it inspires me to go on: "Or we'll bring the federal government down on your pimply ass. You feel *me*?"

Ulrich gives me a nasty smile. "Won't be feeling you anytime soon, dyke bitch. Unless you're planning on switching teams?" He eyes Jeong. "Maybe you switched already?"

All the humor and warmth has gone out of Jeong's face. It's been replaced by an expression that is, frankly, scary.

Ulrich moves aside. He grabs Milly's arm and yanks her away from room 1 as well. "Come on, Milly," he says, "we don't want to mess with Team Psycho. Do we? Boss's orders."

Milly shakes him off. "You really shouldn't be here, Allard."

I sigh and open the door to the room, with Agent Jeong close behind. That wasn't so bad, I guess. I expected to be called a bitch more than twice by this point.

It's a simple white room, just a plain desk and a couple of chairs, along with two not-so-hidden cameras to record interviews (and stream them to the TV in the lunchroom). Neria Francoeur sits at the desk in a defeated hunch, her hands over her face. When she sees us, she says, "Oh fuck."

"Sorry we have to keep meeting like this," I say, and grab the chair opposite her. Jeong remains standing. We're closed in here with Neria, but with cameras recording everything, we'll want to watch what we say.

I've got a lot better light in which to see her this time. Graham's old girlfriend—or old sex partner, at least—has a red, tear-streaked face, but her prettiness still shines through. Those wide, dark eyes, that perfect olive-toned skin. She's dressed in hippie-type clothes, a flowing white shirt and tight flowered leggings. Pale blonde hair tied into two knots. Not the typical murderer look, but I've seen all kinds.

"You told me you weren't working with the police," Neria says.

And there, already, I'm nervous about the cameras. Now it's on record that Neria and I have already met. "I'm not," I say. "But I used to be a cop, so they're happy to let me in to say hi to people. You know, bring in a birthday cake, or inter- rogate suspects in the murder of a college student. It's a special relationship."

Jeong eyes me. I wonder if he regrets this working rela- tionship at all, or resents Marsters for putting him in this position in the first place. It's a tough row to hoe, being a spook.

It occurs to me to wonder *why* the Portsmouth PD picked up Neria and Wallace in the first place. I thought they knew little to nothing about Graham Tsoukalas and who his friends were. I'm pretty sure Mrs. Tsoukalas wouldn't have spilled the beans about the illicit DVD. Though she might have mentioned Wallace and Neria at least as people to contact, if Skip Bradley had pressed her for information.

But how did they nab these two when they were on the run? How did they know where to find them?

The other body, I realize. Or, rather, the *primary* body: Graham's. Had the police found it in the dumpster behind the Tenacious Trainers gym? They must have. And they've probably figured out who the body on Peirce Island is by now, too.

If they *haven't* found Graham's body, though—I don't want to tip them off by mentioning it here. I wish I could ask Jeong if he reported the body in the dumpster to the cops.

"Does the Portsmouth PD know," I say carefully, "about … your other secret?"

Neria's eyes widen. She must be realizing, simultane- ously, both what I'm referring to and my willingness to keep it secret from the police. Because she then chooses her words just as carefully: "No. But you do, huh. Do you know who, uh, that is?"

"I do," I say. "But then I have to ask you, who got dumped on the island?"

Now Neria looks disappointed. Maybe we aren't on the same wavelength after all. "Detective, that's . . . Graham. I told you. It's the *other one* who isn't."

Agent Jeong spreads his hands in a helpless gesture. Maybe he hasn't even seen Graham's body; maybe Marsters sent another agent to check it out. But why would she keep Jeong in the dark, in that case? "Can we stop talking in code?"

I'm not following Neria either—but I'm still following her more than poor Jeong. I pat his shoulder. "Just trust me right now."

Then I tell Neria, "I don't understand. Graham is the one I found. They can't both be Graham."

"They're not," she whispers, her mouth tightening in distress. "Get me and Wallace out of here . . . and I'll help you understand. We'll both help you."

Now Agent Jeong shifts in his seat. "I'm afraid that can't be part of the deal. Divya, I'm not willing to wait—what are you two talking about?"

"Forget it," I say. "We'll come back to it. There's something more urgent we need to know, Neria. About the hole."

At first she looks blank. She doesn't think of it as a hole, does she? Then finally Neria says, "Oh. The gate. The burning gate." She shoots a nervous look at the cameras, but then goes on to say: "You should have left us alone. We were going to close it, Detective."

Just as I thought. "Tell me how." Though it makes me feel extremely silly to ask, I go on with: "Do you need some kind of . . . spell or something to close it? Jeong, get something to write with so we can jot it down."

Jeong, to his credit, *does* pull out a pad and paper. He's as unfazed by my mention of wizardry as Akerman was by the mention of a terrorist cell right here in Portsmouth. With the notable exception of my insane crusade against my own department last year, I'm not normally the paranoid type. You know that. But tonight, paranoia feels entirely justified.

Everyone's reactions are *off*. Everyone around me is holding secrets. I can count myself among them, of course, but I'd still rather we were all showing our hands.

"I don't know if you'd call it a spell," Neria says. A bit uncomfortably. Not a natural wizard, this one. "A ritual, definitely. But it's not just—there are three parts, okay? There's something you need to say. Something you need to do with your body. And some kind of *stuff* you need that gets consumed during the ritual. There's a three-part ritual for every Port, or at least that's what Graham told us."

"Port?" I say.

"Uh, gate," she says. "You know . . ."

"Wait. 'Every' Port. There's more than one?!"

Jeong nudges me. "Let's stay on track. So tell us, Miss Francoeur: what to say, what to do, and what to get."

"It's not that simple," she cries out. "I mean, yeah, you can pick up coal anyplace, and it's easy to walk in a triangle, though you'd need to do it backwards to close the gate. I think. It's the vocal part that's tricky. I only heard Graham do it, and I seriously doubt I can get the sounds exactly right. I'm just . . . fuck!"

She sobs. "I wish I'd never—wish I'd never met him. If I'd only been in a different class that semester, it would've never happened. Goddamn it."

"It's okay," Jeong soothes her. "Just try your best to remember the, uh, sounds, all right? We know you're under a lot of pressure here. This thing is dangerous, though, and we appreciate anything you can give us to help us get rid of it."

His calm, gentle approach works wonders on Neria. So that's what people skills look like. Her ragged breathing slows and she says, "Okay, I'm going to do my best. What I heard Graham say, or, uh, do, was, like . . ."

She makes a noise in her throat. An ugly noise, from a pretty girl. It's kind of like *Krek-kurk-rahk-urkurukka.*

"Hmm," I say. "Wow. We're going to need some practice, I think."

Jeong tilts his head. "Me first." And he gives it a shot. It sounds like *krikka-urkra-kukkuruk.* It's an equally awful sound.

"I guess?"

It's so awful that I have to try it too. "*Kurek, urkarak, kuka—racha!*"

At this point we're all smiling—Jeong because he's an easy-humored guy, and me and Neria in spite of ourselves. Neria says, "Jesus, you're not even trying, lady."

"Sorry. Give it to me again."

She does. For the next few minutes we run through the unholy syllables, but they seem to be changing slightly every time. I don't think we're really *getting* it, but I say with an encouraging nod, "Good. Thanks."

"Keep practicing, guys," she says. "Just maybe not at the gym or the grocery store, okay?" She giggles and then quickly covers her mouth, as if she's shocked herself.

"It's okay," I say. "It's okay to laugh at the horrible and the ridiculous. Cops do it all the time. They have to. It doesn't mean you're taking the situation lightly, or that you don't care."

"Thanks," says Neria. She takes a breath. "So, this is

gonna seem silly too. But can you walk in the path of a triangle backwards? It's probably not as easy as it sounds."

The room is too small to practice this part, but Jeong is determined anyway. He makes Neria get up and then shoves the desk and chairs against the wall. With Neria and me basically flattened against the wall too, Jeong can just barely describe a triangular shape by walking—forward. When he tries going backward, he stumbles over his own feet on the turn.

I laugh. Then I think of the pyramid shape of the temple, and the rough triangle of the hideous, obsidian slug statue. And the mosaic of the flying beasts that surrounded the burning hole (the Port?). It occurs to me, then, that the sounds we've been practicing with Neria aren't far off from the sounds I heard the beasts making. Which makes Jeong's pratfalls seem a lot less funny.

"Okay, give me one more chance," Jeong says. "I feel like I'm trying out for the circus."

That's when the door opens and two of my former colleagues—Ulrich and Daniels—crowd the doorway with guns drawn. They're trained on me, not Ethan or Neria.

"Get down on the fucking floor, shithead!" Ulrich screams.

Not again.

9

The next few minutes pass in a blur. Angry, tense, scared faces surround me as I'm put into handcuffs and hustled away. My old colleagues were pretty pissed at me before. Now they look like I just suffocated their mothers and shit in their cereal.

Ben Ulrich and Burt Daniels bring me to the holding area door. They check their guns into the lockboxes so I can't make a grab for them, and Ulrich scans his ID card. Inside the holding area, Daniels takes my belt and shoelaces, his normally kind face locked in a grimace. His eyes meet mine with a silent question. Since I have no idea why I'm being detained, there's no way I can tell what the question is. I just shake my head. *No* is a reliable answer, I've found.

They lead me to one of the cells. It's a small, windowless cinder block room, painted a cheerful yellow, with a narrow shelf ("cot" would be too kind a word to describe it) and a steel sink/toilet combo. A camera in the corner of the ceiling watches me.

Door slams. I am alone.

They think I'm a monster now. Not just a crazy bitch. And I don't know why. Though I need to *know* why more than anything I've ever needed to know before.

It's a disorienting feeling to look at this cell from the inside.

My old colleagues ignore my shouted questions through the heavy door. And my curses (for it's the perfect time to lapse back into hurling oaths like a Navy man, don't you know?). They leave me in the cell alone for . . . well, I'm not quite sure how long. I don't have a watch, or my phone.

I can take comfort in the fact that they're only allowed to keep me here overnight (though my next stop would be the county jail in Brentwood). In the meantime I've got a stretch of time all to myself to think about what's happened.

It must have been something more than just snooping around and impersonating an officer. More than just finding a body and failing to report it, more than just stalking and trying to make a citizen's arrest in Prescott Park. Maybe: murder.

Do they think *I* killed Graham Tsoukalas? And/or whoever the body on the island was?

They can't both be Graham. Neria's indirect words on the matter, her straining allusions, come back to me now. She acknowledged that I found the body in the dumpster. But she insisted, in contradiction to what I'd seen with my own eyes, that that person had not been Graham. And that the corpse on the island *was* Graham.

Maybe Graham had a twin. They were both dead. No. I'd been to the Tsoukalas house. I would have seen pictures of twins in the house. Mrs. Tsoukalas would have made *some* reference to Graham's twin brother. No, the twin theory was bullshit.

They can't both be Graham. The one I'd found, the

Graham I found, had been missing the one detail that Anonymous Caller insisted on: the wrist implant. (And the only apparent link to you.) Say it wasn't cut out by a medical professional with superhuman powers of incision; say it was never there in the first place. That isn't just a minor detail out of place. That's a huge blow to the concept of the body being Graham.

Neria can't be wrong about Graham. She can't have mixed him up with someone else. She took him inside her, for God's sake.

So let's say who I saw really wasn't Graham. Maybe a cousin with similar features, someone the Tsoukalases didn't yet realize is missing too. Or maybe some kind of freaky doppelgänger from the other side of the world. Greece, perhaps. They say that somewhere in the world, everyone has a twin, someone completely unrelated to them but alike in every way. Isn't that what they say?

Do you have a twin somewhere? Could I find her?

I rub my temples. I feel a hundred years old. I'm so tired right now, I feel like I might actually be able to catch a wink or two on that hideous shelf that only wishes it's a cot. Maybe I should give it a shot, as long as I'm trapped here.

I walk over to it, sit down, and experimentally lie back. I swear I can feel bugs crawling on me.

Anger simmers and keeps me awake. Just who the hell is Anonymous Caller? How dare he get me into all of this in the first place? For a moment, I wonder if the voice was Wallace. No: too different. The voice on the phone was higher, less sure of itself. Even from my limited experience with Wallace, I could tell his voice is both deeper and more confident.

Anonymous Caller said Graham was "our" friend. He'd spoken as a "we." Maybe he'd been a mouthpiece for the

Tenacious Trainers themselves, fellow wearers of the wrist devices. But who was he, specifically?

I come back to the doppelgänger idea. I chew on it, examine it from all angles, the dog on the hunt even while trapped in her kennel. And then I sit up straight. I think I've got this figured out. As crazy as it seems, I think I've got a handle on it.

I'm just drifting off on these thoughts when someone bangs on the little window in the door. It's Agent Ethan Jeong. He enters the cell with a black woman in glasses. She's wearing a smart gray pantsuit and holding a briefcase.

"Allard," Ethan says. "Meet your new lawyer, Barb Okefor."

"It's a pleasure," says Barb, unconvincingly.

I force a grin. "Thank you. Please explain why the fuck I need a lawyer in the first place?"

"There's been a murder," Jeong says. "Er, another one."

"In Prescott Park. Right around the l-last time you were there, Ms. Allard." Barb is clutching the briefcase. She can't manage to smile at me. Am I already a lost cause in her mind? A loss in the columns of her career before the case even begins? "Do you know the name Eric Kuhn?"

My mind reels. Of course I know the name. It's the *Portsmouth Porthole* reporter who delighted in dragging my name through the mud on a regular basis, for months on end. His stories feasted first on the grisly murder of my fiancée, then on my antics and ultimate disgrace. There was a time—let's call it the pre-Kathryn era, because it really does feel like a different, distinct period to me—when I wished he was dead, almost every day.

But I didn't *really* mean it, and I certainly don't feel that way now. Kuhn was just doing his job. He covered major stories for the newspaper; of *course* he had to report on every insane thing that I was doing. Some other reporter would have done so if he didn't.

"Shit," I say. "Yeah. How did he die?"

"Someone bashed his head over and over again against that whale statue in the park," Jeong says. "A witness says— that it was you. Described you to a tee: short Indian-American woman, long black hair, blue scarf, leather jacket, blue jeans. Witness checked his smartphone when calling the police, named the exact time."

My eyes widen. I have this mental image of myself in a mindless rage—like the old Allard, devoid of conscious intelligence, with nothing but emotion at the controls— killing the newspaper reporter in exactly the same unfortunate method Jeong described. Shoving his head into the hard granite of the sculpture over and over again.

What if back in the Sheafe Warehouse, after that unknown assailant attacked me, I got up and . . . sleepkilled?

No! What the fuck, that doesn't make a lick of sense.

"So why do *you* believe it wasn't me?" I say.

"Because by that time of night," Jeong says, "*you didn't have those clothes anymore.* You were buck naked except for my coat."

The lawyer, Barb, looks from him to me uncertainly, uncomfortably. I wonder where Jeong found her. "Maybe we shouldn't be having this conversation here," she says. "Ms. Allard will need to know all of this later on, of course, but I'd prefer that we speak to my client about these matters in a confidential setting."

"Fuck," I say, and then I say it again, shaking my head. Something clicks in my tired, cobwebby brain. What are the odds *another* short South Asian-looking woman would show up around that time, in my own clothes that fit her perfectly, and go on a murderous rampage?

At least it confirms the theory I was just cooking up in my lonely cell. It's a frame job, but I'm now thinking it's not exactly an intentional one. More of a consequence of my own blundering actions. In a way, I really did kill Eric Kuhn. Just not in the way the police think.

"I've got to get out of here," I say.

"I don't know that that's going to be easy," says Barb Okefor. "The Portsmouth PD doesn't have much evidence against you right now, but they're looking to change that in a hurry. They want to get you moved over to county in a matter of hours. And I don't know how your bail prospects are looking."

I press my face against the wall. I'm uncomfortable relying on this lawyer for help since she was handpicked, apparently, by my friends in the FBI. I'd rather not get indebted to them. But I ask, "What can *I* do to help expedite the process of getting me the hell out of here?"

"Lean on your old co-workers here," Jeong says. "Surely you didn't make enemies of *every single one of them*? Have one of them be your character witness and talk to the rest. Someone who can convince them, your old chief in particular, that this witness's testimony against you is patently ridiculous. That you may be many things but you are not a murderer."

Barb swings her briefcase against the sleeping shelf, gently. A kind of nervous tic. "And you need to give us the names of anyone who can serve as a character witness for you outside this department, as well. You need all your allies in a row, Ms. Allard. Think quickly."

I sigh. "Officer Fragonard was my friend, once upon a time. Those days are long past, but—she's got a real internal code of honor. She's the real deal. If there's corruption in this department, it's never touched her and it will never touch her."

"Now, alleging corruption and police misconduct is an entirely separate matter, one that you most likely do not want to delve into given your past record—" Barb says.

"Can it with the legal maneuvering," Jeong interrupts her, not unkindly. "Come on, Barb. The lady's had a hell of a night. She's free to speak her mind right now without us assessing its worthiness as a legal defense."

"This is not the ideal venue for baseless accusations," Barb insists. She looks around nervously, as if she's just waiting for a nearby cop to tell on me. *Chief Akerman, that crazy bitch is still saying mean things about us! Can you keep her on a timeout forever?*

Now, as far as other people in the greater Portsmouth area who'd be willing to stick up for me . . . it's not a super long list. There's Zeke Briard, but he's a slimeball, and if he allowed his true nature to show in court even a little bit, he'd negate his usefulness as a character witness. My parents are too subjective, and anyway, they live back in Manchester—their word would be worth nothing. Then another person does pop into my mind.

"Solomon Shrive," I say. "Young guy who's working at the Friendly Toast. I saved his life with Narcan. His shift's probably over by now, but I'm sure you wouldn't have much trouble tracking him down. He lives downtown. I'll give you the address."

"Shrive?" Jeong says. "That's the witness to the murder."

Oh shit. Everything whirs in my head, trying to make sense. I wish I could get at least a few minutes of sleep. I'm almost ready to tell both of them to go away just so I can do that. But I summon my last drops of energy and say, "We can *use* this. Sol's my friend—he'll jump on any explanation you can provide for what he saw."

He looks thoughtful. "I could bully my way into talking to him."

Out of nowhere, an alarm blares. *Inside* the police station, not outside. I've never heard this alarm before, but I know what it means.

"What's going on?" Barb says, directing the question at me.

I shrug. But I have the notion this is what it sounds like during wartime. When an enemy attacks you on your own turf.

Now I hear gunfire from somewhere else in the station. My heart races. I think my theory's just been confirmed, but I really wish I was wrong.

Milly Fragonard bursts into the holding area. "We're under attack!" she shouts, and she jabs her finger at me. "What in God's name is going on? Is this your terrorist friends?"

"No," I say. "It's me."

They stare at me blankly, but of course there's no time to explain. I just say to Milly, "Can I get the hell out of here?"

I can see Milly waver. On the one hand, she can't see a path to forgive me for what I did to this department, including her. On the other hand, some psycho is attacking the police station. Leaving me shut up and defenseless in a cell isn't exactly the Girl Scout thing to do.

She swings the cell door open wider and jerks her thumb for me to walk out. I do so. My legs feel unsteady and weak, but I'm free. Agent Jeong gives me a dark grin. The lawyer Barb Okefor, on the other hand, isn't pleased to see me on this side of the cell. She hunches behind her brief-case as if it's a capable shield, just waiting for me to live up to my reputation. One crazy bitch, coming right up.

"When we get out of here, I'll need a gun," I shout at Milly over the continuous noise of the alarm.

The smile she throws me is cold and ferocious. "Oh, no. No effing way. I'm sorry, Allard, but those days are *done* for you."

We come out of the holding area. The next burst of gunfire sounds close, ricocheting down the hall. A man lets out an agonized scream.

Jeong grabs two guns from the lockbox next to the door. He's got a Springfield 1911-A1—nice piece. He tosses me the other. It's a 9 mm Glock 26. "Here, buddy," he says, "it's a spare."

I stick the 9 mm in my belt. Not like I'll wave it around right now. Even so, Milly trains her own gun, a very familiar Sig 226, at my face in the next instant.

"What are you *doing*, Jeong?" she shouts. She doesn't take her eyes off me. "Is this how the FBI operates? Handing a firearm to a murder suspect?!"

"She's not a murderer," the agent says. His voice is low but it somehow carries through the alarm blaring. "Pay attention to your gut for just a second, Officer Fragonard. Ignore the playbook and listen to your instincts. You'll know Allard is innocent."

"The heck I will!" Milly snaps. "Get on the ground now, Allard! I'm taking your weapon."

I have my hands up. But I don't move otherwise, except for nodding down the corridor. "*We have to get down there,* Milly. Our friends are dying."

She hesitates and looks in that direction. Her gun wavers in her hand. I could slap it out of her grip with ease, but I don't. We all hear a single gunshot somewhere in the station. Someone cries out, "*Jesus fuck!*"

Milly heaves a huge sigh and lowers her gun. "Come on. But you'll all answer for this later, I promise you."

"I think I'll stay here," Barb Okefor says, bidding farewell with her briefcase as the rest of us hurry down the hall.

I skid to a halt as I spot the bloodbath ahead. Ethan stops just short of crashing into me, and I fling out my hand.

"Back, *back*!" I hiss.

I haven't seen the assailant yet. But Officer Burt Daniels's face is locked in a silent, eternal scream as he lies crumpled on the floor, and that's warning enough. Daniels, who wowed me with his pitching arm on the department softball team. Daniels, who showed avuncular disappointment rather than anger when I blew up at the department. I think I know now what his silent question was in the holding area: *How could you have let things go this far?*

The body of another old colleague of mine, Detective Ken Berger, sprawls nearby. I only know it's Ken because of that bracelet he always wears; the head has been damaged beyond the point of ID. My stomach lurches in horror and disgust.

Milly and Jeong and I crowd into the nearest doorway, into the roll call room, just before a bullet streaks down the hall. That was meant for us.

It's a turkey shoot now, and we're the turkeys. Hell, if there are any cops still left in this fight, one of them might be the one to blow my head off the first time I peek out the door.

Time to get a head count. "Who's in this fight?" I yell. "Anyone?"

"Fuck, she's behind us," someone shouts. Sounds like Gary Piotrowski. Thick neck and bit of a thick skull, but a good heart.

"No, you asshole, I just saw her," I hear Akerman respond. "That's the other one."

"I'm on your side," I call out.

"Then call her off!" the chief screams.

I dare a look into the hallway, clutching Ethan's Glock. I see a face poking out from the doorway to the prosecutor's office, down near the door to the lobby—which is currently propped open by another corpse in uniform. That would be the reason for the blaring alarm. I can see only the legs of that one.

The face down the hall meets my eyes.

And there *I* am. With a Sig 226 of my very own. I'm soaked with the blood of my old colleagues. I must have grabbed the gun off the poor bastard wedged in the lobby door, whoever he is. I've killed at least three so far.

No! Not me. Someone who's wearing my face, maybe, but that's not me. I am right here.

Any observer could be fooled, though. Forgetting my caution, I'm fixated on Evil Allard now. For a crazy moment, I imagine that her movements are tied to mine, like she's my reflection in a mirror. I raise my hand, but no hand answers me. Even at this distance, I can see that she looks like me down to every detail: shoulder-length black hair gathered in waves about a heart-shaped face with eyes wide and dark, prominent nose, jutting-out lips. Dark brown skin.

And, as I expected, Evil Allard is wearing my favorite jacket. She is running what little remains of my reputation far deep underground, where the corpses lie.

A rough hand pulls me backward into the relative safety of the roll call room. Jeong grunts into my ear. "Lucky you still have a head! Jesus. Sit rep?"

I glance at Milly's grimly focused face—she's waiting for my answer too.

"It's me," I say. "Another me. But I think I can talk to her."

Milly shakes her head. "Why did I run to *you* in the first place? I let Daniels and Berger die just so I could spring a crazy woman. What the fuck was I thinking?!" The swear is jarring, coming from her mouth.

"You were thinking you needed an ally," I say. "And deep down, you still want to believe you can count on me. Milly —let me try a conversation with her. Before you go out there with guns blazing and get yourself killed too. She's me and I'm a hell of a shot."

Milly Fragonard raises her hand to me, and I'm half-convinced she's going to whack me. But I don't make a move to defend myself. Her palm lands heavily on my shoulder. It's meant to intimidate, not to comfort, and she leans into me.

"I'll give you thirty seconds," she hisses. "On condition that when this is all over, *you explain everything!*"

"Done," I say quickly, and I squeeze her fingers before I push her hand away.

"Allard!" I call out. Because that's what I would answer to —not Officer, not Detective, not Divya, not Psycho Doppel-gänger. I answer to the name of my mother and father.

"Allard," she says back. I get the shivers hearing my own voice answer me. Okay, not just that: it's hearing my own voice twist and writhe at its ugliest.

I close my eyes, take a deep breath. *Not me. I am me. Not me. I am me.*

I say: "You're angry. I get it. I'm angry too. One of the many things we have in common. But *this is not your vendetta*. It's mine, and it's way past its expiration date."

"They wronged me, all of them, these motherfuckers," Evil Allard screams. It's me in the grip of full-on rage. "These pencil-licking, shit-eating bastards stopped me from finding out who killed Hannah. And then they dragged my name through the mud!"

"That's why you killed Kuhn?" I called out. Just to clarify, just to get it on the record for everyone in earshot. *Her, not me.*

"Yeah, killing that asshat was a good start," she says. "But I came here to get back to the *source*. And if you try to stop me, I'll kill you too, cunt!"

I pause at the novelty of hearing myself call me a cunt. It would almost be funny if literally everything about this situation were different.

"Those wrongs you talk about—they didn't happen to you!" I call back. "They happened to *me*. And guess what, I'm over them."

Now, at least.

She doesn't answer. But I can feel her, specifically her anger, radiating like a wave down the hall.

"You're like a baby," I say. This is partly speculation, but it feels more and more correct as I go on. "You didn't exist a couple of hours ago—you have to start fresh." I gulp, and then say: "Let me help you."

Jeong stares at me like I've just grown another head. (In a way, I suppose I have. There just happens to be another body that goes with it.) Milly tries to get my attention by frantically waving her hand.

"W . . . What?" says the other Allard. And then she falls silent. I dare to hope she's actually considering my words. How much of a *person* is this creature? Is it even possible for her to view herself as a baby? Maybe she's taken it as an insult. But maybe, she's turning it over in her head, discovering that this new perspective could help her.

Then Chief Akerman spoils that possibility by bawling: "*We don't negotiate with terrorists!*"

I peek back into the hallway just in time to see Akerman take a shot at Evil Allard. Imprudently, half of his body has surged out of the doorway to the shift commander's office.

He lands a hit, judging from Evil Allard's scream. Then her scream turns to a roar. Evil Allard, blood streaming down her face, fires twice at my old boss. One goes wide, and that's only because her vision is temporarily obscured by red. The second connects and rips into Chief Akerman's leg. He grips the doorway and falls back into his office.

That's when Gary Piotrowski chooses to break cover from the SWAT office. Not toward Evil Allard, but away from her, toward us, or rather toward the side hallway directly next to us. I'm guessing he got the idea to head for the AR-15 storage locker in the evidence room. An assault rifle would end this quickly enough. I'd do the same if I actually wanted to kill Evil Allard.

But Piotrowski has left himself wide open, even for just a second. He misjudged my—her—twitch speed. My doppelgänger pops out again and shoots Piotrowski in the neck. Screaming, blood spewing from his mouth, the cop joins the pile of bodies in the hall. I draw back, shaken by the execution, which I've just viewed from way too up close.

Jeong is pale and grim. He steadies me. Milly is slower to recover. She just heard a friend die at close range. But I'm impressed to see her pull herself together a moment later, reminding me of the steel that runs through my former friend. Her courage boosts my own, and I can *think* again.

Evil Allard could have killed me as easily as she shot Piotrowski. But she didn't, did she?

"The AR-15s," Milly says. Doesn't she know that was the same idea that doomed Piotrowski? "Give me cover fire, Allard. Only a few steps around the corner, and then I'm home free. I'll get to the locker."

"No," I say. "Number one, you're not any faster than Gary was, and he had fewer steps to take. Number two, we can still do this without killing her. You're not a killer, Milly."

Her face clouds in rage. "Oh no?! My brothers out there are dead. I'll show you just who I am now, *Divya*. I used to think you weren't a killer either—"

"Enough, ladies," Jeong says. Both of us turn to him, briefly united in redirecting our anger. He holds his hands up in surrender. "Whoa. Okay. I just . . . what if we don't do either? What if we stay secured in here? The SWAT team's got to show up real soon."

Out in the hall, Piotrowski has stopped gurgling.

"Would still give her time to kill the chief before they blow her away," Milly says. "No, we have to move *now*."

"I agree," I say.

But on the nature of that movement, I disagree. Before Milly can rush out and get herself killed, I block her by stepping out into the hall. Milly curses me but stays put.

Evil Allard shoots at me immediately. And misses. I have the advantage of being a small target, unlike the big, lumbering guys lying in the pool of gore at my feet—but it still wouldn't be a hard shot. Not for me. There's no way she missed me by accident.

I hear the chief groaning. That's a good sign.

I don't heed Evil Allard's warning shot, nor do I heed her yell: "Stay back!" I keep walking.

I step around the bodies of my old colleagues. I'm shaky with fear, but I get as far as the shift commander's office and then duck inside. Akerman sits on the floor, working on a homemade tie-off for his leg. He raises his gun shortly after looking up at me.

"I told you," I say, "I'm on your side. She's the murderer."

"Fuck your whole family," Akerman says. But he lowers his weapon, grimacing.

"We'll sort this out," I say with more assurance than I feel.

I've got to take the next step now or I'll chicken out. I've been off the force for too long, immersed in the mundane world of vandals and loiterers and misplaced ID cards at the JIA security desk. I've gotten used to that soft feeling of *not* placing myself in death's path.

I call out: "I'm coming over, Allard. Let's talk."

"I'll shoot you for real this time," she says. "I swear."

I march out of Akerman's office and across the hall, flinging myself into the prosecutor's office. I'm flying against every instinct of self-preservation that I've regrown in the past year, and it feels good.

It's a shock to see myself up close. Evil Allard is leaning against a chair, bleeding copiously from her ear. She holds her hand to her face, distracted by her own pain. It occurs to me that I could kill her, after all.

It would be safer for everyone. It would end tonight's body count with an exclamation point.

But—call me a solipsist, but I don't have it in me to blow away someone who looks exactly like me. Especially since, when I look at Evil Allard, I *do* see a baby. A big, angry baby, yes. But, if my theory is right, she's still a newborn to this world, one lacking the life experience to develop a conscience of her own. The blame for her actions rests on her parents: the late Graham Tsoukalas and myself.

All she is right now is a collection of my own worst emotions. Out of my ignorance, and my deep-seated flaws, I created her. I won't now destroy her.

Instead, I grab a big stapler from the desk and chuck it at her head. Evil Allard doesn't get knocked unconscious—that would be too simple, too easy on me—but she does get thrown onto her side. The 226 falls from her hands.

I jump onto Evil Allard and force her against the floor. I shove her gun a safe distance away from her and then toss away my own as well. She offers only token resistance. She's trying to catch my attention.

"Chief shot me," she was mumbling. "I have to kill him. Chief shot me. I have to . . ."

"You had it coming. Stay still."

I hear a rush of footsteps approaching. Evil Allard, though her head must be ringing like an alarm clock, squirms underneath me in a renewed burst of energy. She almost throws me off. She's strong, like I'm strong. Maybe stronger. Maybe she hasn't paid the toll of broken bones and moderate alcohol abuse and all the other insults I've inflicted on my body over the years (so much for the "body is a temple" theory). Divya Allard 2.0.

Her elbow comes up and knocks me in the chin. I reel back, my face tingling, but now I have help. Agent Jeong and Officers Fragonard, McLaren, and Prince crowd around me with all their guns pointing at the wretch on the floor. She keeps struggling anyway, as if she wants to die by cop.

Then Jeong and Milly, as if they've signaled each other, simultaneously drop down on Evil Allard's wriggling body and keep her down while Milly slaps handcuffs on her.

"What are you doing?" sputters Officer Mike Prince. He makes a jerking motion with his handgun. "All of you assholes, move out of the way and give me my shot!"

"Going to shoot a woman in handcuffs?" Milly asks him. Sweat trickles down her wild-eyed face, and she looks like she could start screaming at any minute, but she's not budging from her position. "Don't think that's in the manual."

"She killed Burt and Gary!" Prince screams. "Get out of the fucking way, bitch!"

Officer McLaren, breathing hard, looks almost as turbulent as Prince does right now. But he gets himself together and puts his hand on Prince. "Easy, Mike. Easy! This isn't who we are."

Prince snaps a hateful glare at McLaren. I know the look, because I know the man: a racial slur is likely on his lips. He chews on the words in his throat, then swallows them and slumps in defeat. He lowers his gun and steps back. "Fuck it, you all can take care of this. I got to call an ambulance for the chief."

Milly stares at me as he stalks off. "Prince won't be the only one. Your sister, here, is going to get strung up Wild West style by a bunch of angry guys tonight if you don't have a plan. Now tell me everything!"

Jeong nods at her, all warmth and professional courtesy now that the crisis is over. "Thank you for your help, Officer Fragonard. We're going to give you the explanation you deserve, by and by. But right now—my people need to take this clone, or whatever she is, into custody."

He's said the strange word at a low pitch, so that only Milly and I, and possibly McLaren, could hear him. Milly looks at me for a long moment. Finally, she shows me her palms, backs off, and guides McLaren away to the shift commander's office.

I have a feeling we're still not best buddies. Maybe we'll never get there again. But I've got bigger issues to worry about tonight.

On trembling legs, I stumble out into the hallway. I can finally focus on the body wedged in the door to the lobby. I open the door wider. The glass case of memorabilia in the lobby has shattered. The front half of the body is lying in the glass, gun missing, giving credence to my idea that this was the guy who unwittingly armed my doppelgänger.

It somehow doesn't surprise me to see that Evil Allard's ticket into the station was Officer Skip Bradley. He'd be just stupid enough to let her trick him into "capturing" her, thinking that he had the situation under control right up until the second he didn't. But I've spoken enough ill of the dead.

THE PARKING LOT is full of emergency vehicles and sound and light. The SWAT team has arrived, belatedly, along with police cars from the neighboring towns of Kittery, Newington, and Greenland. About a dozen guns train on our little party of me, Agent Jeong, and the captive Evil Allard before we can consider sneaking out.

As we kneel on the pavement with our hands above our heads (well, Evil Allard with hers still handcuffed behind her back), Jeong shouts at the cops to check his pocket for his FBI badge. Once they do so, they let us up. They have strong reservations about letting us leave the scene with the murderer in tow, but Jeong promises them we'll be back. His badge can move mountains, as can the mere mention of his boss, SSA Marsters.

The cops do keep staring from Evil Allard to me and back again, understandably. *One twin sister is evil, and the other isn't? Doesn't that only happen in soap operas?*

I can only imagine what the city council must be thinking right now, Stone and all her well-heeled cronies. Tonight's body count is a little bit enormous, isn't it? They must be ready to kill me with their bare hands just for the damage I've done to this year's tourist season. I wouldn't want to be in Akerman's shoes tonight when he gets the first call.

Eventually we're on our merry way. They even let us keep both of Jeong's guns. Though I can sense Jeong's trepidation at the piles of paperwork that will await him after tonight's adventures. At least that's one duty I've escaped, having been stripped of my own badge long ago.

Evil Allard is silent as we walk toward Jeong's car, picking at the bandage on her ear. But I'm full of stuff to say, for once, forgetting my own loathing for chatterboxes. I'm too amped up to stop.

"So I guess I don't need a lawyer anymore," I say. "But do you think Evil Allard does? What kind of interdimensional jurisdiction do you guys have? Oh shit, and speaking of the Port, do you really think we've got this ritual down? Should we make a pit stop for some coal? Do you remember the—"

"Stop." Jeong opens the back door and shoves the unresisting doppelgänger inside. "We need to take this one step at a time. *First,* we need to get this—thing—into a safe place, where she can't hurt any more people. A specialized place. I happen to know one, because of the, uh, specialized nature of my office."

He eases into the driver's seat. It'll be a short ride to Daniel Street from here, but as soon as Jeong starts driving, he forgets his plea for me to shut up. Curiosity wins out, and he says: "Now. You didn't seem at all surprised to face down an exact duplicate of yourself. Give me the abbreviated version: what the hell happened tonight? Where did *she* come from?" He jerks a thumb at the backseat.

"You ready for a story?" I say.

Did I know Graham Tsoukalas? No. It's too late for that. But I can give you my best guess at a sketch of the kid's life.

Graham was a thoughtful guy, a dreamer, a philosophy major. An open-minded lover. The big questions tugged at him, as they begin to do for most people of college age: what are we doing here? Is this all there is? If not, what's out there to find? For most of us, these questions remain unanswerable, because we're stuck in our orbit of the ordinary. But someone gave Graham Tsoukalas a key to a door, behind which an answer might just be found. How could he resist?

Who knows who it was. Someone from the Tenacious Trainers? I'd like to find out, but let's focus on Graham right now, our intrepid seeker. Armed with knowledge from an unknown source, he went to open this door to elsewhere. Were Wallace and Neria there for the first opening? I don't think so, not from what Neria told us. I see Graham as the kind of guy who would want to check out the scene all by his lonesome, at least at first. Remember the "Backup" DVD: he didn't fully trust his intimate friends.

So he stole out to Prescott Park, probably at night, and went into the Sheafe Warehouse. He performed the ritual: speaking the weird words, walking a triangular pattern, and flinging coal at the designated spot. And then the door—the Port, let's call it, since that's what Neria said—opened.

Cue his first glimpse of that *other* place. Graham wouldn't have walked through, not then. He probably closed the Port again in a hurry. I'm sure he had no fucking idea what he was doing. As would be the same for most of us, messing with gateways to other universes. The difference being, I think most of us would have the sense *not* to mess with said gateways, especially not more than once.

But Graham was a seeker. He might have been terrified the first time, but his mind eventually came around to the idea of opening the Port a second time. This time, he would have to walk through. He would have to see what was out *there*. But maybe he didn't want to do it alone.

So his fellow bedroom explorers Wallace and Neria got an invitation. Maybe they were all having one of those late-night dorm room conversations that seem so consequential, and Graham turned to them and said, "There's a *place* I need to show you." And the words he then spoke, combined with the utter seriousness on his face, gave his two lovers grand dreams of the possibilities that lay ahead.

Tonight, the three of them waited until dark fell and the crowds thinned. They sneaked into the Sheafe Warehouse. For the second time, Graham performed his little ritual to open the Port. But if he was hoping for them to accompany him through, he would end up disappointed: Wallace and Neria were simply too terrified to even approach the thing, never mind step through it.

Maybe they begged him to stay away from it, too. But Graham was determined. He'd already made up his mind, and with an audience he *had* to go through with his exploration.

On the other side, Graham found a strange temple devoted to a giant slug. Became awed, moved, inspired, etc. He'd brought his sketchpad, because Graham Tsoukalas had a touch of the *artiste*, and so now he sketched that mosaic of the flying beasts and the statue on the altar. Then he put the sketchbook down to investigate the rest of the temple.

He next saw what *I* saw: all those windows with a prime view of a hellacious landscape. The pairs of scary, inter-twining flying beasts maybe smelled him the way they smelled me, and they made their approach. Graham's journey of wonder and discovery turned in a heartbeat to pants-pissing terror.

He fled back into the inner chamber of the temple. In his panic, he forgot about his sketchbook still lying on the altar. The only thing he could think about now was escape. Graham ran for the Port.

And sure, Graham made it back to our world—but something came back with him. Something that looked just like him. The major difference was that it was butt-naked, the way Graham himself came into the world twenty years ago. Free of clothes and wrist implants alike.

I know, sounds crazy, right? Well, how about a gateway to another universe? That's fucking normal?

Evil Graham was a walking manifestation of the original Graham's worst impulses. Apparently one of those impulses was self-destruction, because Evil Graham attacked his progenitor almost immediately.

I'm thinking Evil Graham possessed a frightening amount of strength. At the very least, he had a reserve of willpower that Graham didn't. He saw an opportunity for a new life, but he'd have to put someone else out of the picture first. Graham fled from the warehouse, over the bridge to Peirce Island. Evil Graham was probably hot on his heels, otherwise why make the poor choice of heading for a dead end?

Sadly, in the final confrontation, Evil Graham won out and killed Graham. He then stole his clothes. After all, the dead Graham Tsoukalas that the police found was naked. That detail was mentioned in the initial version of Kuhn's *Porthole* story before the police censored it.

Wallace and Neria were too paralyzed with fear to stop what happened. The Port alone probably was enough to freak them out. So when this malicious doppelgänger came through after their friend, attacked him, and then chased him, they just stood by and watched. They were too chicken to follow Graham and his twin out to Peirce Island, otherwise their bodies would have been lying there in addition to Graham's. Or there'd be *two* Graham corpses side by side. No, they ran away instead, which gave Graham's evil doppelgänger the time he needed to change into dead Graham's clothes.

But Wallace and Neria still weren't safe. Evil Graham came after them next. Given his desire to take Graham's place in this world, he was intelligent enough to realize he had to kill the only other two people who knew of the Port.

So he drew upon Graham's imported memories of Wallace and Neria, and he tracked them down. He caught up with them outside the Tenacious Trainers gym, which they had probably run to for answers, like I had. A showdown ensued. Together, Wallace and Neria were able to overpower and kill Evil Graham, though the experience must have been a nightmare. They then stuffed him into the dumpster out back. This was probably happening around the time I was talking with Christine Figueroa at the Friendly Toast.

Our poor two kids realized that there was no way they'd be able to explain the presence of two dead Graham Tsoukalases, never mind one. They decided to run. So they went back to their apartment and packed their bags. But Wallace and Neria also grabbed the coal Graham had used to open the Port, in the hopes of closing it before they flee. They'd failed to help their friend—but their consciences wouldn't let them leave the Port open to perpetuate further murder and mayhem.

Trouble was, I was there to interfere. I grabbed Neria and caused Wallace to run off. Then, in the confusion, Neria ran off too. Then I got the fool idea to go into the Port.

When I came back, I *brought my own Evil Allard back with me.*

She came into this world naked, just like Graham's doppelgänger had. Spontaneously generated, somehow, by the Port itself. And just like Evil Graham, Evil Allard wanted to usurp me—though I suppose my suicidal tendencies don't run as deep as Graham's did. Because Evil Allard didn't want to kill me. Not then, and not at the PD either. She just sucker-punched me and took my clothes.

Disguised as me and fancy free, Evil Allard embarked on a campaign of revenge. The targets: everyone I hate, even today, despite my new "enlightened" self forged through months and months of therapy. It's like my id grew a pair of legs. Evil Allard embodies all the ugly stuff that still lurks underneath the surface of me.

[Here, *Evil Allard feels compelled to interject from the back seat: "Is justice ugly? Is it ugly to balance the scales?"*

"Shut it," I say. "When I want my opinion, I'll give it to me."

"Maybe the real ugliness is cowardice," Evil Allard says, her

eyes glittering, as she leans forward. "Just imagine if you'd had the courage to do what needed to be done—last year. Strap Henry Akerman to a chair in a dark room and you'd know who killed our Hannah soon enough."

I take her by surprise. I take her by the throat. Only Jeong's bark of command stops me from squeezing.

"Get on with it," Jeong says coldly. "We've been sitting here too long."]

Evil Allard's first big break was to run into Eric Kuhn, *Portsmouth Porthole*'s star reporter, who'd returned to Prescott Park to follow up on details about Graham Tsoukalas's death. She didn't hesitate to slaughter him, to mash his head against the whale statue, because she honestly believed she hated him to the point of murder.

Because of me. Because of the anger and hatred that I've still been harboring in my mind, all this time.

Meanwhile, Wallace and Neria had returned to the park, to try one last time to close the Port. Conscience and guilt still motivated them, even after my blundering interference. Unfortunately, they didn't even make it close to the Port this time. The cops, who have wised up to potential suspects after the late Skip Bradley's interviews with the Tsoukalas family, nabbed them right away. We know they didn't reach the Port because the cops haven't yet discovered it.

Then Evil Allard moved on to her next target for revenge: the Portsmouth police station, full of cops who let us down and potentially covered up a murder, then shamed us and fired us for wanting to know the truth. And that idiot Bradley was her way in. She would have murdered them all if we hadn't stopped her.

But let me say it again: Evil Allard isn't responsible for her actions. She may be a murderous monster, but—I don't believe that's all there is to her. I don't believe that's the extent of what she can be. The truth is, we know *nothing* about how that Port operates, therefore we know nothing about this little asshole's true nature.

That leaves me with one question: what is the FBI planning to do with her?

12

J eong's look of intent listening fades as I turn the question on him. "You say you've got a place to 'store' her. But what do you intend to *do* with her? I'm guessing the FBI's interest in an extraterrestrial clone would go beyond mere containment."

The agent shrugs. We've pulled into the McIntyre Building lot on Daniel Street and Jeong has his hand on the door handle. "You've got me, Divya. Tonight's the first time I even knew an extraterrestrial clone, as you put it, could even exist."

No, you *used the word "clone" first,* I think to myself. Jeong's deflection hardly seems sincere. I say, "*Wait,*" and the agent refrains from opening his car door.

"Did you guys *know* about the existence of Ports?" I ask, my face growing hot. "Your little office of curiosities, funded by—what was it—Project Stargate?"

He smiles, though it's not so charming this time. "We . . . had a suspicion. Nothing solid. Tonight was the first time I've ever seen one."

"Maybe you could have told me about your suspicions

before you guys sent me out to stumble into strange alternate universes!" For the first time, I'm truly angry at Jeong. I guess I'd lulled myself into thinking he might actually be my friend. But no, just another cog in the wheel. "Or did you *want* me to create a killing machine copy of myself?"

"I'm still here," Evil Allard says from the back.

"We didn't know," Jeong says. "We were 90 percent sure the Ports were a fairy tale. Or at least I was."

I note this subtle blame shift onto his boss, and it doesn't mollify me one bit. "This is bullshit, Jeong. Would you send a fellow agent into danger without giving them every piece of intelligence you knew, even the '10 percent chance' stuff? I don't think so! Crazy old Divya, on the other hand? Well, fuck her, I guess, she doesn't even carry a badge anymore. Expendable."

"Hey," Ethan Jeong says. "Hey." The concerned look on his face just pisses me off more. Don't tell me he's scared now. Does my current expression eerily match the one on my twin's face as she gunned down Portsmouth's finest?

"You and your whole office can go take a swim in the goddamn Piscataqua," I growl. "Right after you all give me the answers about Hannah that you promised me."

"You're an idiot if you think they're gonna tell you a damned thing," Evil Allard remarks.

I glare at her. "That's *enough* out of you, Body Snatcher. One more fucking word—"

"Divya," Jeong says, holding up his hands. "Please. I would have *never* let you go out there if I knew about the danger you'd be in. Believe it or not, I took this job to protect people, not to sacrifice them to extraplanar monsters. I should've stuck with you from the moment you made your deal with SSA Marsters. I'm ... sorry."

My anger wants to keep raging. But a glance back at Evil

Allard is enough to make me feel sickened and exhausted, and slowly the anger drains back down into its dark reservoir. "To be fair," I mutter, "I wouldn't have tolerated a babysitter anyway. I would have shaken you off before we even reached the Tenacious Trainers gym. I know how to lose people."

"You certainly do," Evil Allard says.

I take a deep breath. She can't hurt me if I don't let her.

"I promise," Jeong says, "it'll be full disclosure from here on out, Divya. Everything we've learned from the Stargate initiative will be yours to peruse. You've earned that much after what you've been through tonight. Just let me talk to—"

His phone rings.

As he answers the call, it occurs to me Evil Allard is still wearing my jacket.

"Take off my jacket," I command. I lean into the backseat and encourage her by yanking on the collar.

"All right, I get the message," Evil Allard mutters. She wriggles out of the jacket and I pull it into the front with me, slip it on, and pat the pockets. My phone, my wallet, the dead kid's sketchbook: it's all there. Miracles do happen. Oh, *and* the DVD of Graham and Wallace doubleteaming Neria. To think that almost ended up in the slippery hands of the police and therefore the media.

I have several missed calls and a voicemail from Sol Shrive. I'm guessing he was rather confused about what he saw tonight.

But I don't get the chance to listen to the message. Jeong rings my internal alarm as I hear him say: "Stay there. Keep guarding the Port. I'm headed up to the office now." He hangs up. "We've got a huge problem."

"Even huger than our other problems on this most fasci-nating of evenings?" I say.

"I'm fucking serious," Jeong says. He jumps out of the car, and I follow suit.

"Allard, stay here with your evil twin," he barks at me.

I shake my head. "Uh uh. You *just* told me you wouldn't be shutting me out."

"No. This—this is different—"

"And you clearly don't have time to argue with me," I say. I pop open the back door and grab Evil Allard by the cuffs.

"Fine," Jeong snarls. "If you let her escape or harm anyone, I'm sending both of you to containment."

"Yes sir."

He hurries up the three flights of stairs. I follow at a slower pace, keeping a close eye on the other Allard the whole time. She won't catch me unaware with a sudden kick or a strategic dive and dodge. As it happens, Evil Allard doesn't try. She plays along for now.

I catch up with Jeong in the main room of the FBI office. He's staring in shock at a figure lying on the floor amid a carpet of knocked-over papers. It's Agent Ramirez. The woman is groaning in pain, blood pouring down her temple. She momentarily focuses on the two of us through the haze of her head wound but says nothing. Her eyes flick in the direction of the next room.

I say: "Ethan, what—"

He brings his finger to his lips. Then we all hear the noise from nearby. Three voices—three incredibly similar voices—are all chattering and barking orders at the same time.

"Jesus on a cherry popsicle," Jeong says, paling. He unholsters his gun and rushes in.

13

Three SSA Kat Marsterses are busy at work in her office. None of them are naked, thankfully—she must keep a couple of extra outfits in her closet—but the sight of them still unnerves me. One's on a cell phone, another's on a desk phone, and the third is sitting at Marsters's desk typing furiously at her computer. The two on phone calls are having Very Important Conversations, mostly involving the Marsterses shouting curses and commands in alternating order.

"No, you *must*," says Cell Phone Marsters. "I can't just wait around for you to see this thing. Once you see it, you'll be convinced, but we need additional personnel here at once."

"And resources," Desk Phone Marsters says, temporarily holding her own handset away from her head.

"Yes," Cell Phone Marsters snaps at her, "I was *getting* to that part. Get back to what you were doing. No. Sorry, wasn't talking to you. But resources. This represents an innovation in defense technology that will make Bob shit his pants. *Literally.* The possibilities are ..."

Meanwhile, Desk Phone Marsters is saying, "... insubordination. Yes. Recommend an immediate demotion and transfer for Agent Ramirez. Of course, I can hold ..."

Defense technology. Oh, no. No, no, no. I did *not* unearth that Port just to hand it to the military. That's one area where I happen to agree with you on the subject of authority. Even as a lowly beat cop, I could get a whiff of how the military operates. Bunch of large adult sons who never outgrew their toys. I can imagine a dozen different ways for the Department of Defense to abuse the Port for their own ends. Cloned soldiers is only the least of it.

I keep a firm grip on Evil Allard, who wears a look of bland indifference at this scene, and I glance at Agent Jeong. He looks horrified, but that's no guarantee he'll be with me on this. I sure hope this situation doesn't get any uglier than it is now.

I rack my brain trying to remember which outfit Kat Marsters was wearing earlier tonight, so I can figure out which one is the real deal. But I've got a shit memory for clothes. It looks like I'll have to rely on logic instead: would I ever hand *my* smartphone to someone else to use?

I throw Jeong a signal, pointing at the one on the smartphone, and he nods and then waves frantically at her. Even in a situation like this, he's unwilling to shout and interrupt his boss(?) on the phone. But he does hiss at her in a low decibel: "Agent Marsters!"

"Hold on," this Marsters says. "I'll have to call you back."

She hangs up. "*Well?!*"

"'Well?'" Jeong repeats. He's turning red. "Forgive my impatience, Agent Marsters—I've been in a deadly firefight tonight—but *what do you think you're doing,* messing with interdimensional technology? And what did you do to Ramirez?"

The Marsters on the desk phone says, "Hold on, I'll have to call you back," and slams the handset into the receiver. She points at Agent Jeong. "You're out of line. Don't forget who you're talking to."

"I don't *know* who I'm talking to!" Jeong sputters. "Can you please tell me which one of you is the original Kat Marsters?"

The Marsters at the computer stops typing and says, "Punish him."

"Arrest him," says the Marsters who was on the desk phone.

"Agent Jeong has been a loyal team player for years," says Smartphone Marsters. "We're cutting him slack—for the moment. But he should carefully consider this warning not to question our judgment. *Are you considering it, Agent Jeong?*"

Chastened, Ethan Jeong straightens up and says stiffly, "Yes sir. But I must register a formal protest at your actions."

Really? That's it?

I finish strapping Evil Allard to a sturdy-looking heating pipe along the wall with a second pair of cuffs. I feel secure enough about my handiwork to join the conversation. "He's too 'loyal' to say it, but you've gone around the fucking bend, lady. My own doppelgänger, here? She just killed a journalist and four cops. She would have slaughtered the whole department if we hadn't stopped her. You don't know what you're doing."

"It's true," says Evil Allard, helpfully. "Your sisters may look like you—but they're just babies."

Jeong glances at both me and my doppelgänger. I can't tell whether he appreciates the assistance. But I'm afraid his working relationship with SSA Marsters will continue to taint the conversation. I need to take control here. After all,

I've been promised an answer about what happened to you, and I intend to get it. Even the glare I'm getting right now from all three frightening Marsterses won't dissuade me.

"Was this your plan all along, Marsters?" I ask, focusing on the smartphone one. "Find the Port, start exploiting it for the government, no matter the human cost?"

"You have never known the weight of national security on your shoulders," says Desk Phone Marsters.

"If you think the United States can afford to hesitate at exploring any new strategic advantage—you are a child," says Computer Marsters.

"Quiet!" says Smartphone Marsters—or rather, Marsters Prime. She *must* be the original Marsters, because both of her twins have instantly shut their mouths at her command. They must all have an ingrained deference to authority, which serves Marsters Prime well.

"It is highly annoying to have someone else arguing on my behalf," Marsters Prime goes on. "Even if that someone else is myself."

The laugh that bubbles up in my throat dies just as quickly. Maybe this would be funny if it wasn't so horrible. I wonder what the extent of Kat Marsters's powers are as a supervisory special agent. Probably not much beyond this office. The way she's talking, she must have greater ambitions—much greater. Now she has the means to climb that ladder.

Maybe at the expense of the rest of us.

"We owe you no explanation," Marsters Prime says. "But we thank you for your service."

"How about the answer you owe me?" I snap. "I figured out who killed Graham Tsoukalas: his own clone. Now who killed my fiancée?!"

She smiles at me. "Of course. How could I neglect our

bargain? Very well. Our findings indicate that someone within the cult of Port-openers must have murdered Hannah Ryder."

"But—" I say. "That doesn't make sense. I thought she was *part* of that 'cult.' She had one of the wrist thingies just like the rest of them."

"There are . . . disagreements within organizations all the time," says Marsters Prime, shooting a look at Agent Jeong.

He takes that as a cue to step in and steer us back to Marsters's indiscretions. "Sir, our task is *not* to capture new technologies for the United States. That's the DoD, or hell, DARPA. Our designation as a 'strategic office' doesn't change that. We're just here to keep people safe and neutralize any—unusual threats that other agencies overlook."

Speaking of annoying. I'm in this up to my eyeballs now, so I want my good buddy Ethan to stop talking in code around me. I need to know what this field office has really been up to.

"Your naivete strikes us as willful, Agent Jeong," says Marsters Prime. She circles around her desk. Agent Jeong flinches. But he doesn't step back even when she gets right in his face (or rather, right below it). "First of all, *your* task is to do whatever the fuck we tell you to do. Second: why do you think we're given Project Stargate resources?"

Jeong stays quiet.

"Heh," Marsters goes on. "To 'keep people safe and neutralize threats.' Do you think the U.S. government is as passive as all that? We are ever hungry for new advantages over our enemies—who grow more numerous by the day."

She grabs Jeong's chin and forces his gaze downward, into hers. "You're out of the loop, kid. So don't pretend you know what's going on. Trust those of us who do. Do we have any reason to question your loyalty?"

"No sir," Agent Jeong says. Then he adds, "But my loyalty is to the people of the United States, not to you. I believe this is an abuse of power and a danger to the public." My respect for him shoots from somewhere on the first floor to up through the roof.

"Then you are suspended from duty," Marsters snaps.

"Give us your badge!" says Desk Phone Marsters.

"Give us your gun!" says Computer Marsters.

Marsters Prime shoots them an annoyed look and adds: "What they said."

"Don't do it," I say. I step forward. Evil Allard will be okay on her own for a moment—I hope. Adrenaline courses through my body. *Hello, old friend, I thought we'd seen the last of each other tonight . . .*

"Fuck you," says the SSA. She draws her gun, a Glock 17M, and fixes it on me. The other two Marsterses step out from behind the big desk. "Get down on the floor, Divya Allard. This doesn't concern you. I thank you for your part contributing to the defense and security of the United States, but your role in this is over."

Jeong looks panicked. Despite the defiant stance he's just taken, he doesn't intervene on my behalf. I get down on the floor. I'm out of options.

"Hand me your gun and badge, Agent Jeong," says SSA Marsters, "and do it *now* before I shoot your new girlfriend."

"You do know she's not into guys, right?" Jeong says, stalling for time. "You've read her file?"

Marsters releases the safety and stands right over me. She points the gun barrel at my head at a distance where she can't miss in any universe of probability. The other two Marsterses now flank Jeong.

He sighs and hands his gun to Desk Phone Marsters and his badge to Computer Marsters. Marsters Prime makes a satisfied sound in her throat and says, "Me Number Two, now take Officer Allard's pistol away from her, if you please."

Computer Marsters moves toward me. Once she has my gun, all three Marsterses will be armed, and this fight will be past any hope of us winning. Maybe Marsters Prime has benign plans for me and Agent Jeong. I find I'm not willing to take the chance.

I risk a tiny glance up at Marsters Prime, who has relaxed her grip on her gun. She's fully confident that her twin will take care of disarming me. A truly stupid idea thus enters my mind. I'm probably going to commit suicide by FBI agent, but I'm out of options.

Sure, I got the beginning of an answer for what happened to you. But it's not enough, and the source couldn't be less worthy of my trust. *I need to know more.* Your fate is one mystery I am absolutely unwilling to leave unsolved when I leave this Earth.

So that's when I wriggle onto my side, quickly draw the Glock 26, and shoot Marsters Prime in the ankle.

I can't say I have any idea what it feels like when a bullet tears through old-lady flesh and bone. I just hope I never experience the sensation if I ever make it to Kat Marsters's age.

Her Glock 17M drops from her hand as she screams and falls to the floor. I reach for it at the same moment Computer Marsters lunges for me. We collide, and the impact knocks me away from the 17M. Advantage Computer Marsters. She's still on her feet, and I'm still on the floor. Still have my 26, but hesitation at shooting the clone in cold blood costs me my only advantage.

At that moment, Evil Allard, chained behind me, lashes out a foot and connects squarely with the face of the Marsters clone. Computer Marsters stumbles and drops next to me.

I struggle to my feet, throwing my doppelgänger a confused look of gratitude. She just nods at the 17M that Computer Marsters never reached. I scoop up the gun. I kick the Marsters in the side, wincing as I do so, to make sure she stays down.

Ethan Jeong has used the moment of confusion to his advantage in the meantime. Desk Phone Marsters lags behind him in reflexes, so she failed to defend against a vicious chop Jeong dealt to her wrist. Jeong's Springfield 1911 falls from her grasp. Jeong dives for it while she's still nursing her injury, and by the time Desk Phone Marsters lumbers forward, Jeong is already spinning to put the barrel against her forehead.

Finally, all three Marsterses are unarmed and under our command. It hardly feels like a moral victory, though, beating up and cowing three aging women at gunpoint. I glance back at Evil Allard. She's smiling at me. I don't smile back. "Thanks for, uh, the assist," I say.

"I preferred to bet on you over the psycho triplets," Evil Allard says. "By the way, I see you're double-fisting—I'd be happy to hold one of those Glocks for you."

I ignore her and refocus on our captives. Marsters Prime and Computer Marsters are huddled together on the floor, their arms around each other. Jeong still has his Springfield trained on Desk Phone Marsters, who is upright but standing stock still. *What a mess.*

"You little fools," says Marsters Prime through gritted teeth. "I would've spared you."

"Says you," I reply.

"Where are the keys to special containment?" Jeong asks. "Your desk?"

Marsters Prime spits at him and misses.

"I'll take that as a yes," says Jeong. He circles the desk and rummages in the top drawer until he finds a ring with three large brass keys on it. The keys are *glimmering* strangely. I blink twice and look at the keys again; the slight disruption of the air around them remains.

"What is *up* with those keys, Jeong?" I say, alarmed.

The agent bites his lip. I hope he's thinking about his promise to me back in the car. No more bullshit, just answers. "They're biplanar," he says finally. "We've got a guy who—prepares the keys for special containment. Someone the agency discovered through the GRILL FLAME experiments. Lock and key both exist partly here and partly someplace else."

"Shut your *mouth*," Marsters Prime says.

I rub my face and try to understand what Jeong just told me. My brain is already overloaded for the week. "You're gonna have to run that by me again."

"Listen, I don't fully grasp it myself." He jangles the "biplanar" keyring at me. "Right now we've got four people to lock up. Not far to go, just down the hall. Let's start with the Marsterses."

It's too late to ask this, but I ask it anyway. "Are you sure you've picked the right side?" I say. "I'm grateful, of course, but this is probably the end of your career with the FBI."

Jeong gives me a sour laugh. "Hardly. We're nothing like your local PD. The Federal Bureau of Investigation *rewards* agents who weed out the incompetent and the dangerous. I'll probably get a promotion out of this, if I don't get a bullet in the back of the head for knowing too much."

"Remember I helped," says Evil Allard.

"Duly noted," I say. "Stay *right here.*"

We shepherd Marsters Prime and her twins down the dimly lit hall until we reach a big steel door I didn't notice before. I guess I never got a tour of this whole place. The door's double locks both shimmer in the same way Jeong's keys do. I cover our prisoners as Jeong fits the locks on the door with two of the biplanar keys. Then we invite the three Marsterses inside ahead of us.

A row of giant steel cubes makes up the special containment area. Ten or twelve cages altogether, each with its own biplanar lock. One by one, we stow each Marsters in her own steel cage and Jeong uses the third key to turn the lock. As we escort Marsters Prime into her cage, she wheezes at us through her pain: "This is treason against the United States government!"

"I don't think they'll see it that way," Jeong says with a smile, and closes the door on her. Then he adds, "Don't worry, Kat, I'll make sure a medical professional shows up eventually to get that ankle treated. Just sit tight."

Once we've sealed up special containment again, I look at Jeong. "So you told me you thought the Ports were just a fairy tale. And yet you guys set up your own little supernatural Guantanamo right here in Portsmouth. Square that for me."

"Marsters supervised the construction," Jeong says. "At the time, I didn't know why. All I knew was that someday we might host prisoners who'd need . . . uh, some extra reinforcement. With our designation as a Project Stargate-funded field office, we're supposed to be prepared for threats to come from unusual quarters. So we received an SOP to follow from specialized researchers in the agency, working with adepts like the biplanar lock system guy."

"Specializing in what, multiple dimensions?" I ask.

"Those keys and locks—they've got that in common with the Ports themselves, don't they? They connect one place with another."

Jeong cocks his head at me. "I suppose they do. I suppose I should've connected the dots, knowing about the keys already. Still, it's a big leap from weird keys to whole gates that people can cross through."

"But Marsters knew about the Ports, even if you didn't," I say. "She didn't hesitate to step through one. *Twice,* since she made two clones of herself."

"Right," he admits. "She kept a lot from me. She must have had more information from the researchers than I was privy to, leading her to believe that we *would* discover a door to somewhere else, sooner or later."

"And that once that door was discovered, you people would take full advantage of whatever lay beyond it," I say. "No matter what the cost."

"You're talking about Marsters," Jeong says. "She was clearly off the rails. I already told you, *I'm* focused on protecting people. I didn't join the Bureau blindly, Divya. I went where I thought I could do the most good."

I could argue with him further. After all, the Marsterses seemed to have *many* parties within the agency who were interested in hearing from them. But Ethan has been through hell tonight, most of it because of me. I just don't have the heart to beat him up for his boss's sins, not when the most vital question remains unanswered: "So who was Marsters talking about? In the Port-opening group. Which one of them killed Hannah?"

Jeong opens his mouth to answer me. "Honestly, Divya, that's yet another thing Marsters was keeping from me. I don't—"

And then we both see the steam uncurling from the

open door to Marsters's office. We hurry inside and peer through the steam cloud, both of us cursing to ourselves in frustration. I guess the pipe wasn't as sturdy as it looked. Or Evil Allard summoned a last, desperate reserve of strength. Either way, our fourth prisoner is gone.

14

First things first. We tend to Agent Ramirez with the office first aid kit. Her head wound isn't as bad as it initially looked; heads just typically bleed a lot. She's coherent enough to say, "Please tell me you got that crazy asshole and her new twins."

Jeong nods. "You were brave to stand up to them alone. But you could've gotten yourself killed."

"What he means is, thanks," I put in.

Ramirez nods at me. "Thank *you*. The papers were wrong about you, Detective Allard."

"Well, duh," I say. "Did you see their election coverage?"

Agent Jeong makes some administrative calls to clean up the growing tangle of loose ends we've generated. Of course, we've still got a final task tonight before either of us dares to sleep, and that doesn't even include finding my evil twin. As soon as he puts his phone away, he turns to me and says, "Let's go."

"What about Ximena?" I say, nodding at his colleague.

"We have our own doc, and she's on her way now," Jeong says to me. "I just updated McGuinness and Barnes on the situation. They're going to keep guarding the Port until we get over there. Barnes mentioned she already turned away a couple of Portsmouth cops suspicious about what was going on. We don't have much time before they complain to another agency and break up our party."

Motion forward is a good thing. We hop back into his car. As we make the short drive over to the park, I say, "I'm worried about another killing spree."

"Yeah," he says. "I'm hoping you got through to her. In any case, I've got people looking out for someone of your description—in your old clothes, of course, but I'd also like to keep the cops from arresting *you* again by accident."

"Thanks," I say. I grab Graham's sketchpad out of my jacket and flip through. At the back, I find what I'm hoping for: two sets of phrases in the same strange tongue Neria tried to articulate for us. I stare at them, feeling my mind twist as it wrestles with the language. I realize after a moment that the first set is for opening the Port, and the second is for closing it. Neria only told us the opening phrase, which makes sense, because she never got to see Graham close the Port.

I speak the crackling syllables of the closing phrase aloud.

"Hey," Jeong says. We've parked in front of Prescott Park. "Knock it off, you're making my head feel weird."

"Sorry, just practicing." Now that he mentions it, my brain feels a little funny too. Maybe I shouldn't use these words when not in the vicinity of the Port.

I get out of the car. My phone buzzes. It's Sol. Shit, I forgot to listen to his voicemail, but there's no time now. I ignore the call. I need to focus on closing the door to the twinned-serpent hellscape, but my brain keeps jumping back to the problem of my MIA clone. Where would I go, if I were not me but still me?

Maybe the better question to ask is: who else was on my mental hit list, before therapy helped me get over it?

Evil Allard's rampage left a lot of cops alive. She could track down any one of them to their homes (or to the hospital, in the case of Chief Akerman). Since I know where most of my old colleagues live, I'm sure she does too. My heart curdles at the thought of Evil Allard darkening Milly Fragonard's door. After all that Milly did to help us back at the station, that would be a fine thank you indeed.

And who else? Somebody who cut me off in traffic once? A telemarketer? My anger isn't always based on reason. In fact, most of the time, anger is an unthinking beast. Now that beast is running around cloaked as a person, liable to strike out at anyone or everyone in this city. *I did this.*

I have to stop thinking about her before I go insane. Jeong swats my shoulder and says, "Come *on.*"

Then I see Sol Shrive running across the park toward me.

"Oh, thank God, Divya!" he calls out. Then he slows down and halts a safe distance away. "Hey, it . . . it is you, right? The real Divya? Please tell me it's the real you!"

"It is," I say. "It's okay. I'm not a killer."

My friend comes closer and dares to give me a hug. Jeong gives me a curious look. I pat Sol's back and disengage.

"Some seriously weird shit has been happening tonight," says Sol, apparently uninterested in my companion. "So Eric—you know, reporter from the *Porthole*—he came by the Friendly Toast. Wanted to know about Graham Tsoukalas, poor kid. I didn't know Graham, but I knew he was part of this weirdo exercise cult, the Tenacious Trainers.

And I also knew his best buds, *intimate* buds from what I hear, were Wallace Riggs and Neria Francoeur . . ."

Damn. If I'd confided in Sol when *I* encountered him at the Friendly Toast earlier tonight, I could have saved myself a lot of headaches. I wouldn't have needed the FBI to rescue me from the late Skip Bradley for one thing—*oh well, fuck it.* I couldn't have known. But now I look at Sol with newfound respect, at least as a source of useful information. "And then Eric Kuhn went haring off after Wallace and Neria?"

"Yeah," Sol says unhappily. "My bad. I cut out of my shift at the Toast early after that. I'd started thinking maybe it wasn't a great idea to let Eric go off alone into the night when there was a killer on the loose. I called a ride to take me to Islington Street where those two kids lived, but on the way I saw Eric in his car, coming back toward town! I—"

"This has got to wait," Jeong breaks in roughly. "I'm sorry."

"Just one sec," I say, holding up a finger. "So you followed him back to the park. And saw 'me' kill him and then you called the cops."

Sol's face is pale at the memory. He nods. "But that wasn't you. I *knew* it. Do you have a sister?"

Jeong taps an invisible watch on his wrist and looks at me pointedly.

"No. Or not that I know of. My parents only adopted one kid. She's—listen, this killer is still on the loose." I leave out the fact that she was briefly *not* on the loose before we lost her again. "Now Agent Jeong and I need to find her before she can kill anyone else."

I turn away, Jeong's face relaxes into relief, and then Sol cries out: "That's what I wanted to tell you! I would have if you ever answered your phone!"

"Oh, my God," the FBI agent hisses.

"I know where she is *right now*," Sol babbles on. "I just got a call from somebody who knows somebody who lives on South Street. The second somebody saw you in the neighborhood. Walking into the cemetery."

"You could have *led* with that part," I say. "OK, now we *really* have to go!"

"Wait, I'm coming with you," he says, and Jeong groans. "I can't let another person die tonight. You might need backup."

"*I'm* the backup," Jeong says. "You're a civilian with no weapons."

Sol Shrive gives him a strained smile. "There's a lot more I need to tell Divya. Vital stuff. Please just let me come along."

I'm not going turn him down this time. "Fine, but let's hurry. And you have to do everything we say."

Jeong and I climb back into his car, and Sol crawls into the back seat. Hopefully McGuinness and Barnes can keep people away from the Port for just a little while longer; collaring Evil Allard in the cemetery is our new priority. Jeong checks in with his colleagues on the phone as he drives. Meanwhile, Sol chews my ear off:

"So this isn't a long-lost sibling situation. Or you having a split personality. I bet it's your, uh, evil double. I think during extreme emotional stress, under the right conditions, in the right places, *our shadow selves can be made flesh*. My great-uncle wrote a story like this once, and it was fiction but he was, like, going off established occult sources. It's totally supported by paranormal researchers. It's like we're tapping into this emotional plane just behind our reality, and—"

"No," I finally interrupt him. *Please tell me this isn't his "vital stuff."* "No, Sol. Or not really. It's—I'll try to explain when this is all over."

Will I? I don't know if it's wise to keep indulging Sol's curiosity. Then again, he already knows enough to get himself in a heap of trouble.

We park on Richards Avenue, across from the entrance to the South Street Cemetery. As we walk past the enclosed yard at the corner of Richards and South, I look for the two sheep who live here, but I don't see them. They must be tucked away in the shelter for the night. Rommie McNair, former Portsmouth mayor and current sheep- and goose-keeper, is my best guess for Sol's somebody's somebody. I wonder if she's watching us right now.

We walk through the ancient gates of the cemetery. It's vast and dark. The graves up front date back to the 1700s, when Portsmouth was the happening spot in New England to trade spices and slaves from the Caribbean. There are thousands of graves here spanning the centuries. But tonight I know exactly where to go. I motion for Jeong and Sol to follow me, navigating by the light of our phones.

The moon comes out from behind the cloudbanks to reveal your gravestone. But Evil Allard is nowhere in sight.

"Damn," I say. "I really thought—"

Then Sol lets out a strangled cry. I whirl to see my double with her cuffed hands around Sol's neck. She must have sneaked up behind him. The handcuff chain squeezes against the soft flesh of his throat.

Ethan Jeong has his Springfield up in a flash, though he knows as well as I do that he's more likely to hit Sol than Evil Allard. I leave my gun in my belt and take a soft step toward her. I say: "Hey. You."

The extra pair of handcuffs is still hanging from my double's cuffed hands. It clanks as she turns to me. Evil

Allard's face is set in a despairing growl that gives me the shivers. "Tell me who I am, Divya Allard."

"You're my anger," I say. "Just like the Marsterses were her ambition. And Graham's clone was his suicidal impulse."

"Not good enough," she seethes. "I'm not the fucking embodiment of an emotion. I am a person. Sure, a *very angry* person—but I'm still a person!"

I'm at a loss. I don't know whether she really deserves personhood. She's a manifestation born out of a gateway to another dimension. And an evil one at that, too.

But hell, I guess if corporations can be people, then Port-spawned doppelgängers can be too.

"Okay, you're a person," I say. "But you don't get to be *me.* There's already one of those."

"I can't—can't draw the distinction," Evil Allard says. Her voice is uneven with panic. "You filled me up with these horrible feelings, these *instincts.* Bad memories. Prejudices. Vendettas. But where's all the good stuff? I thought coming here would help. Thought Hannah could help me find something worthwhile inside me. I've been *trying,* but I just feel . . . nothing."

"You never got the chance to love Hannah," I say, softly. "I did. Maybe love doesn't transfer like hate does."

Evil Allard bares her teeth at me. I cringe away from the sight of my own twisted, feral face. "Well, fuck you very much for the rotten gift. Now what am I supposed to *do?!*" She screams the last word and yanks the handcuff chain against Sol's throat. He makes a choking sound. I can see tears on his cheeks, reflecting the moonlight. But to his credit, he doesn't beg for his life, doesn't utter a word at all.

For the first time, I wonder if that pipe in Marsters's office was old and weak after all. I was able to physically subdue Evil Allard back at the police station, but . . . is she getting stronger? Should I be worried now?

"Just say the word, Divya," Jeong snaps. "She's gonna kill this kid."

Hearing an implied *anyway* at the end of Jeong's sentence, I immediately say, "Do *not* shoot!"

Then I refocus on my twin, trying to make my tone as soothing as possible. "Let me help you. You can't figure this all out alone."

"You were going to put me into 'special containment' at the FBI office," she says, thrusting a finger at me. "You were going to *ABANDON* me. Don't pretend that you're my fucking friend now, you backbiting, crotch-kicking whore."

"I won't abandon you," I say.

I mean it, because I have to mean it. Being *me*, she'll see right through me otherwise. I go on: "Please, Div . . . Divya, or Allard, or whatever name you'd like to choose for yourself. Do you want my middle name? Benazir, how does that sound?"

She doesn't respond. But neither does she renew her effort at choking the life out of Sol.

"Please come with me," I say. "We'll need to restrain you, but I *promise* I won't abandon you."

For a moment, I think I've actually gotten through to her. She relaxes her pose and searches my eyes, eyes that are hers too. Then the blind demons of rage that pushed her to kill five people now seize her again and stiffen her. She says, "*No.* I won't go into restraints. You can't imprison me for your own crimes. I'm walking away, Allard."

"Not with Sol you aren't," I say. "Let him go."

"Then your agent friend shoots me."

"*He won't,*" I say. "Right, Ethan?"

"Goddammit, Allard," he says. He doesn't lower his gun.

We're at a standoff that only I can break. My thoughts race. I find, in my heart, I don't truly believe that Evil Allard would kill someone whose life we—I—had already saved once. Sol is *probably* not in real danger. She probably wouldn't hesitate to kill Ethan Jeong, though, if she had the opportunity. And Ethan may not hesitate to kill *her* if Sol gets out from between them. Someone is going to die if I don't act.

"Take me instead, then," I say. "I'll be your hostage." Slowly I draw the Glock from my belt and lay it in the grass, so she can see I'm now unarmed.

"Allard, if you do this . . ." Jeong says.

"Don't pretend you'd shoot me, Ethan," I say. "I know you at least well enough to know that. Put your damn gun down."

He exhales an angry sigh and then lowers the Springfield. I wait until I've gotten close enough to Evil Allard—Benazir?—to block his shot, then I say, "Let Sol go."

My doppelgänger lifts her cuffs enough for Sol to escape. She lifts her eyebrows at me. The fact that I don't know the true extent of her strength and speed is enough to hold me to my word; I won't risk losing a fight and letting her go after my friends. I turn my back to her and let her slip the cuff chain over my throat.

I suppose this is the moment when I find out whether, like Graham, I have any deep-seated suicidal tendencies after all. With one hard squeeze, Benazir could snuff out both of us.

"Pick up the gun, kid," Jeong hisses. I watch Sol awkwardly scramble for the Glock I dropped. But he doesn't point it at us. And Benazir seems unconcerned; like me, she probably knows Sol could never pull the trigger.

"Where you going to go?" I ask Benazir. "You want to

walk, so where exactly are you going to go? You have no ID, no money, no accounts. With no past, you have no future. You can't have *my* past, because this time there's no way you can pass for me. Far too many witnesses back at the station."

"I'll figure it out," she murmurs. "We can improvise. We're good at that."

She tries to move, but I plant my feet. The chain presses against my throat, and I see black spots. "Hey," I gasp. I grab the chain and hold onto it. "There is no 'we.' I'm not going to help you with a damn thing if you run. But if you give your-self up—I'll be your ally. I'll make sure nothing bad happens to you. You hearing me?"

I listen to Benazir's ragged breathing for a few seconds, hot against my ear. Finally she says, "You're no *ally* of mine."

"I'm your only friend in the world," I mutter. "Just look at their faces. That's how everyone will look at you, for the rest of your short life, unless you let me help you."

I let her process my words. I keep up a steady glare at Agent Jeong so that if he decides to shoot, he'll at least be looking me in the eye when I die. Then, finally, the pressure at my throat releases. Benazir Allard lifts her arms and frees me.

I wait a beat before turning back to her, just to show her how unhurried I am to act. I see that my twin has sunk to her knees. Gently, I crouch in front of her.

"Shoot me," she growls. "I'd rather be dead than a monkey in a cage for the rest of my life."

"That won't be your life," I say.

Ethan Jeong draws near with his gun trained on Benazir. "Divya," he says quietly, "don't make her promises that you can't keep."

"I haven't," I say.

Sol comes over and hands me the Glock, looking glad to

be rid of it. He rubs at the red flesh of his neck as he gawks at Benazir. "You sure this isn't your shadow self?"

"She was created by a gateway to another dimension," I say. "So no. This isn't a psychological concept, this is . . ." I look at her. "A person."

"A person who is definitely going into special containment," Jeong says.

"Let's talk about that in a bit. For now we should hightail it back to the Port. We have to close that thing before anyone *else* decides they need a clone or two."

"With her along?" Jeong responds sharply. "Do you really want to risk another Houdini act? Or are you planning to stuff her back through before you close it?"

"*No*," Evil Allard says from the ground.

"No," I say. My tone is, I'm hoping, definitive. "She'll behave now. She understands her situation."

"Fine. What about Sir Tagalong?" says Jeong. I don't get the veiled hostility. He can't be jealous?

"I humbly request to accompany you there, m'lord, m'lady," says Sol, grinning and bowing. "I'd like to see what a gateway to another dimension looks like, if you don't mind. I'm not saying you *owe* me, but . . ." He rubs his neck again.

I admire his resilience after nearly getting strangled by a handcuffed madwoman. But I still feel like wiping that grin off his face.

"Okay," I say, "if you're ready to get scared out of your gourd. You might just wish she choked you to death after all."

15

———

We arrive at the Port not long later. Agent Jeong held onto the shopping bag full of coal briquettes that Wallace and Neria dropped at the warehouse, and now I'm carrying it. Jeong and Sol are close behind me. Benazir Allard walks beside them, as docile as she promised to be, though that doesn't stop Jeong from sweating.

We step into the Sheafe Warehouse, where two agents await us. One is a stocky black woman in her mid-thirties with tied-back curly hair and a crooked smile. The other is a taller white man approaching fifty; though he's lost most of his hair, with the remainder going to grey, his face is remarkably unlined for his age. Had it not been for his wrinkled, bony hands, I might have assumed he was younger. I assume they're Lena Barnes and Mike McGuinness, respectively.

I'm relieved to see that, unlike their boss, neither Agent McGuinness nor Agent Barnes has been tempted to go through the burning hole and create evil copies of themselves. Progress!

"Jesus, I hope you guys are ready to close that thing," Agent Barnes says by way of greeting. "I keep finding myself staring at it—into it—kind of mesmerizing. One time McGuinness called out to me, and I realized I was taking very slow steps toward it."

"So just to be clear, *nobody* has gone into it?" Jeong says.

"Correct, Ethan," says McGuinness. "We've kept both the police and lookie-loos away."

"Great, good work," Jeong says.

"You mind telling us who this is?" Barnes says, indicating Sol, who is agog at the sight of the burning hole. The young man tilts his head, trying to look at it from a different angle, just like the rest of us have all done. Unlike the rest of us, though, Sol doesn't seem scared by the Port in the slightest. In fact, he walks right over to it.

"Hey, Sol!" I say sharply. "Watch it around the interdimensional thingies, will you?"

"This is—*spectacular*," he says. "I mean, all the rumors I was hearing about the Tenacious Trainers . . . I thought they were just your run-of-the-mill Satan worshippers. But *this* is the real deal. If I'd known, I would've . . . um, I ever tell you about my dabbling in psychogeography, Divya?"

I shake my head, bewildered. "Psycho-what?"

"Psychogeography," Sol repeats patiently. His eyes reflect the flicker of the ghostly flames. "The mapping of the *mind* of a place. You take a place like Portsmouth—you bet your ass it's got its own mind. Its own soul, even. And I don't mean in, like, a metaphorical sense. All of us, through the centuries, we build the mind of a place. Through what we bring to it, and what we leave behind. It gets to thinking on its own. And you can *communicate* with that mind if you walk through the place in the right way. Without purpose, without direction. Let yourself walk through Portsmouth with no destination, and you'll start to hear the voice of the city itself."

"I see why you never told me about this hobby," I say.

"I know, sounds fucking crazy, right? And, okay, my most perceptive walks all happened to involve a large dose of fentanyl. But still. I *heard* things that only the city could tell me. Secrets. As far as I'm concerned, this gateway represents a *conversation* that Portsmouth is having with another place. Maybe cities get lonely if there's no one there to understand them."

Sol's ranting is unnerving me. "That may be the case," I say, "but it's time for this conversation to end."

"Wait." Sol interposes himself between me and the Port. "Are you *sure* you have to make this thing go away forever? Right now? Someone should be studying this. Just think of the possibilities if we could actually control gates like this. What if we could go wherever we wanted to in the universe?"

McGuinness barks at him to back off, and Sol listens to McGuinness, at least.

The agent adds, "You're thinking along dangerous lines, son. Not that I have any doubt that our top brass in the agency would be thinking the same way, but—that's what led the boss astray. We could destroy our own world trying to reach other worlds. Officer Allard is closing this Port, right now."

I hesitate. McGuinness is right about the potential for abuse of power—Marsters is Exhibit A, B, and C—but Sol's plea for someone to study this Port phenomenon is not entirely off base. A qualified scientist, perhaps one of the FBI's "specialists" Jeong referred to, could learn a lot from this gate. The quest for knowledge and the quest for power may intersect at certain points, but that doesn't mean they're the same thing.

Still—fuck this Port. It's done.

A trickle of sweat runs down my temple as I open the bag of coal. I'm supposed to throw pieces of this stuff through the Port while chanting the words described in Graham's sketchbook, pronouncing them with those horrible growly-clicky sounds we practiced with Neria, and walking backwards in the path of a triangle.

At this point, it's really late at night. I'm bone-tired. I'm having vivid fantasies of my bed back in my apartment on Pleasant Street. The last thing I want to do is perform a stupid and complicated arcane ritual, in front of an audience, no less. But it's time to bring this nonsense to an end.

"Just, I better not hear any ridicule from any of you guys while I'm doing this," I say. "Can't have anything throw off my game. You need to absolutely shut the fuck up. Agreed?"

They all nod. Sol looks a little intimidated. Maybe he's flashing back to Evil Allard smashing Kuhn's head into the whale statue over and over again.

And speaking of Benazir, she looks a little wistful at the Port. I guess I might be too if I were about to see my birth-place disintegrated.

"Okay, here goes," I mutter. I position myself just a few feet in front of the Port and begin my awkward backward walk. I hear that alien wind whistling again, just like last time. *Don't look too closely in there. Don't think too closely about what you saw in there.*

I start in with that guttural inhuman string of brittle consonants, adhering closely to Graham's notes. "*Kuhh-harkkhack Kaahhuhhrk — Uhhrraggh — Kahhahrakur . . .*"

Now the tricky part. I have to keep up those sounds, and I have to keep backward-walking, while I fling some coal briquettes into the hole. God, am I still remembering to make the reverse-reptile sounds? *Kuhharakk Kahhrraahhkuh Uahahhrraghh Kahhhahurkk Kuhkuharrhhh . . .*

Nobody's laughing at me. Each briquette dissolves as soon as it makes contact with the Port. I have the uncanny impression that the Port is eating the coal. And the false fire starts to flicker. The Port gets smaller.

I hear a roar from the other side, followed by a terrifically vibrating sound, like an avalanche rumbling down a mountain. I realize that it's not snow and ice tumbling down, but the basalt bricks of the temple. Grey stones and dust rain through the small field of vision that the Port affords me. Through the chaos, I think I see the obsidian statue of that giant slug rocking on its pedestal.

They smell me. Even through the Port, they smell me.

"Shit!" Jeong says. "Hurry up!"

And *that* doesn't help. But you know Divya Allard is a stone-cold trouper, so I keep making the growling, crackling sounds even under pressure, even as I feel ready to piss my pants at the sight of the twinned silhouettes snaking through the ruin. Two pairs of gigantic, yellowed eyes make a direct course for the shrinking Port. The wind over there is so loud with the sheltering temple walls now fallen.

No, you bastards. No—

An enormous, scaled, dark-brown snout thrusts through the Port. Its nostrils exhale steamy clouds. I scream and jump backwards, stumbling. Everyone else is shouting too. The beast's mouth struggles to open, but the confines of the Port won't let it.

However: I've stopped my recitation. I'm no longer walking the backwards triangle walk. And to my horror, I see the Port slowly begin to enlarge once more. Soon that scaly mouth will have enough space to open, and we're all pressed against the warehouse walls, knocking framed paintings to the floor. We'll have nowhere to go but outside, and that'd be giving up—

A shot rings out, earsplitting in the confined space. Agent Barnes's bullet deflects off the hard scales of the snout and buries itself in the wall just above my left shoulder.

"Divya, *finish this!*" Sol shrieks.

I steel myself. I check Graham's notebook, still clutched in my sweaty hand, one more time, and then I resume the incantation in that horrible alien language. I don't have enough room to walk the reverse triangle anymore, but I pelt the snout with coal briquettes.

The Port closes tightly around the snout—quickly, as if it'd been impatient for me to get back to the ritual. And then the beast lets out a terrible close-mouthed squeal as the Port continues to diminish, cutting through its scales and the flesh and bone underneath as easily as, well, slicing through peanut-butter pancakes at the Friendly Toast. (My stomach churns.) The snout blackens at the area of contact with the closing gate.

And then, with a distinct lack of ceremony, the Port collapses into nothing and the heavy, severed snout thuds to the warehouse floor.

We're all silent. Finally McGuinness says, "I'm not cleaning *that* up."

I slump to the ground, suddenly feeling exhausted. Barnes goes to my side. "You okay, kid?"

"Yeah . . ." I mutter out of a voice far too croaky and dry to be my own. Barnes lets me have a few swigs from her water bottle. She's a nice lady, for a professional liar and sneak.

Sol joins me on the floor. He's shaking all over, but his eyes are bright with excitement. "That was just—I—wow.

Man, this is all just like something my great-uncle would write about . . . That place on the other side sure looked *cyclopean* . . ."

"Okay, okay," I croak. "Sol, I'm still waiting for that 'vital stuff' you had to tell me. I don't want to hear any more theories about emotional shadow planes and chitchat from the secret mind of cities. I need concrete information about the Ten—"

"Hold on," Sol says. He looks at the three FBI agents. "Not here. Somewhere more private, if'n you don't mind. No offense, esteemed federal enforcers of the law."

I shrug. "Agent Jeong, would you mind bundling Benazir into your car and bringing her back to the McIntyre Building?" I see their confusion at the name, so I hurriedly amend myself: "My clone, I mean. Sol and I will meet you there. Should only take us a few minutes to walk."

Now it's Jeong's turn to hesitate. He must hate the thought of missing out on inside information—no matter what it's about. Hazards of the trade. But then he sighs and says, "Fine. Get some fresh air. Just don't collapse on the way, Allard—you're looking pretty hollowed out."

If I stumble, I'll always have Sol to pick me up again. That's what friends are for.

The severed snout has begun to stink: eau de carcass left on the grill too long. Barnes says to McGuinness, nodding at the dead meat, "We'll flip for it. Winner goes with Ethan, loser coordinates the cleanup and coverup."

"Fine, but *my* coin this time," McGuinness grumbles. He pulls a quarter from his pocket and calls heads in the air. Then, scowling at the results, he says, "C&C of *this* is a two-man job. You better hurry back, Lena."

Benazir nods at Jeong and Barnes, indicating that they won't have to manhandle her, but they do anyway. We exit the Sheafe Warehouse with them and they take off at a jog through the park, Barnes clearly eager to get moving after her long guard duty. Sol and I walk in a different direction. Once Sol and I are alone—with nothing resembling a Port in sight—I breathe out my relief.

Now that we've parted from all traces of supernatural interference, I have a momentary fantasy about just heading to the Press Room and drinking away the memories of this night.

But I did make a promise to Benazir, and I intend to keep my word. Guess I'm funny like that. I want to know what exactly they plan to do with the creepy little psycho—and I'm going to have a say in the matter.

I offer my arm to Sol. He accepts it. We're just two friends out for an evening walk in the park.

"Sorry for the detour," says Sol. "For my friends' sake, I'd rather not share any more information with the Feds than I have to. I don't trust them, and neither should you."

"Those Feds have given me a ton of help tonight," I say. "Ethan in particular is far braver than his job description requires. But let's have our chat. How much do you *know* about the Tenacious Trainers?"

"Beyond the gym itself?"

"Yes. Obviously."

Sol Shrive leans in close. "A little. I mean, that—Port back there took me by surprise. Like I said, I thought their little cult was just a bunch of overgrowth Goth kids. I didn't know they were doing anything *real*. So when they invited me to join, I respectfully declined."

"They *asked you to join?!*" I say, taken off guard. "You could've mentioned that—So you know who they are, then? The people who are in the group?"

The night seems to be closing in on us. We're already to

the construction site at the end of State and Daniel Streets, where they've been working on the new Memorial Bridge that will reconnect Portsmouth to Kittery, Maine. We'll be at the McIntyre Building in no time. I slow my pace and Sol is forced to as well.

"I mean, yeah, some of them," Sol says. "If you go to the gym itself, you can see who's working out there, though obviously not everyone who goes there to exercise is a member of the cult. It's a subset. The ones with the wrist gadgets."

"You keep calling them a *cult*," I observe. "Why? Graham doesn't seem like he was a particularly religious person." *And neither were you, Hannah, with all your talk of "false gods"—though maybe you were looking for a real one?*

"There are all types of religions, Divya. Me, I worshiped at the altar of chemically induced good times. You're an acolyte of the truth. And these people . . . they sure talked like cult members. All this stuff about 'finding nirvana' and 'opening the doors of the universe.' At the time, I didn't know they meant it literally. So . . ."

"So if Graham Tsoukalas was fixated on opening a Port," I say, "maybe the other Tenacious Trainers cultists were trying to do the same thing."

And maybe they succeeded. It's the larger implication that my mind hasn't wanted to face tonight. Somewhere in this city, there might be other gates to that nightmare world, or even to *other* places, irresponsibly thrown open by a dozen other young fools just like poor Graham.

"*Right,*" says Sol in excitement. Unseemly excitement, in my opinion. His voice grows louder. "It's clear to me now! They know exactly what they're doing. Maybe they have secret meetings in the back room of the gym, sharing information about how to open Ports." He looks wistful now.

"And I turned 'em down. I could've been an interdimensional adventurer all this time . . ."

I glance around. It's the middle of the night and nobody's around, but Sol's making me seriously paranoid. He's not exactly being discreet with all this stuff, and we're practically right outside the federal building. "Don't shout," I hiss.

"Sorry," Sol says.

"Someone told me tonight that the Tenacious Trainers were the ones who killed Hannah," I say. "Which would certainly be odd, because I'm 99% sure they're the ones who put me on Graham's case in the first place. But you're the one who's met them. You say they seemed fanatical. *Are they capable of murder?*"

His eyes widen. He hesitates to speak, and I grab his arm. "Be straight up with me, Sol," I say.

"N-no," he stammers. "Listen, Divya. I only met two of them. A girl around my age, and a guy somewhat younger. They seemed kooky, sure, but killers? No. I don't think so."

"Their names," I command him. The blood is rising in my cheeks.

He stares at me. Courageously, he doesn't break eye contact. I see a guarded aspect hood his gaze. "Divya," he says. "I can't do that. You're just going to give their info to your FBI friends, and you have no evidence they've done anything wrong."

I let go of him. I know he's right. Marsters's word alone is too thin to go on. And yet I would happily see the lives of strangers turned upside down by federal agents if there were even a tiny chance of finding justice for you. My days as a former paragon of law and order have never seemed more distant.

I take a few deep breaths to calm myself, and then an

idea strikes me. "Sol," I say. "Can you do me a favor? Well, two favors."

He looks at me cautiously. "I owe you all the favors in the world, but—"

"First," I say, and I take the DVD out of my jacket pocket and hand it to him. "Hide this somewhere safe. Don't watch it. Just hide it."

He nods, confused. "And second?"

"Tell those cult recruiters you've reconsidered," I say. "Tell them you're ready to find nirvana."

16

W hat I've been able to dodge so far, mentally, is a simple corollary: if the Tenacious Trainers are a cult, then you were a cultist too.

But that's impossible. It *has* to be. You would never hide something from me that huge.

Would you?

I always knew you kept parts of your life hidden from me. Whole swaths of your past, for example. I got the feeling demons had taken up permanent residence in the Ryder household, and so I didn't pry. I also didn't ask about where you'd been during those nights when you would disappear for long stretches of time. I didn't want to be The Jealous Woman, and besides, my own job often meant crazy hours and added stress for you as well as me.

I wanted to cut you some slack. My free-spirited girl. If you didn't stay at least a little mysterious, I wouldn't have as much fun with our relationship, would I? Maybe I liked the manic pixie dreaminess of your tendency to come and go.

But . . . if *this* was what you'd been up to—not just inno-cently, intensely working out, but also meeting with loons and crackpots about how to *open gateways to other universes* ...

And you felt you couldn't share this with me? Not even just a little? Not even the tiniest goddamn clue about the deepest desires of adventure in your heart of hearts?

If you'd ended up going through a Port—would you even want to take me with you? Or would you have just disappeared?

I may never know what ends you pursued. But with Sol infiltrating this, ahem, cult, I can at least find out if your pursuit ended you.

The door to the McIntyre Building is unlocked. I enter, alone. As I'm about to head up the stairs, two FBI agents I've never seen before (I'm *assuming* they're FBI agents) come down hustling SSA Kat Marsters along with them. She's in handcuffs and looks pissed, especially because she's hobbling. At least someone treated her wounded ankle; it sports a fresh bandage and splint.

"Don't think this is the last time you'll see me," Marsters says dryly to me as they reach the foyer. "Not like this."

"Hey," I say. The agents pause but look irritated. "Where are you taking her?"

"None of your business, ma'am," says one of them, a tall, bald black man. He shows me his badge. "Agent Harriman of the FBI Boston Field Office. This is government business."

Well, at least I've determined they aren't some *other* shadow organization. And Agent Harriman basically answered my question anyway. I shrug and let them haul Marsters off.

I ascend the stairs like an old woman. I need rest. By the time I reach the doors to the resident agency office, I'm breathing rapid and shallow breaths, and I'm holding on to the wall so I don't fall over. Quick deterioration. I wonder how much of myself I gave to close that Port; after all, one of the elements was the triangular movement of my own body.

McGuinness and Barnes greet me at the door, both looking concerned. Barnes says, "Come on, girl. Get yourself over to this chair and sit a spell."

I'm tempted, but I say, "Nah. If you could let me lean on you a bit, though, and take me to Benazir and Agent Jeong, that'd be great."

McGuinness gives me an appraising look. "Well . . . sure. They're down at special containment right now. With our boss's boss, Assistant Special Agent in Charge Mark Ivanov. From the Boston office."

"Help me get over there, then," I say, too tired to conceal my irritation. Why are these two acting so cagey? Is it because the big boss is in town?

McGuinness cedes responsibility for me to Barnes, who does take my arm. She escorts me down the hall to the big steel door, which is currently standing open. When Barnes tells me to watch the slight rise in the floor as we walk into the special containment area, that's enough to make me snap, "I see it!"

Barnes's smile falters. "Of course you do, Officer Allard."

"Eh. Sorry." I reclaim my arm. "I think I'm feeling better, thank you for your help."

Two agents stand in front of the steel cages. One is Jeong. And the other is a pale man with his collar loosened and tie missing. Lank brown hair cascades to his shoulders. Not my idea of a honcho, but maybe when they reach high rank they get to ignore the haircut regs. This must be Ivanov.

"Evening, gentlemen," I say, offering my hand to the pale, long-haired man. He gives me a limp, clammy shake and a brittle smile. "ASAC Ivanov, I'm former police officer and current security guard and transdimensional traveler, Divya Allard."

"Oh," he says through his teeth. "You're one of the funny ones. Agent Jeong, have you been getting along with Miss Allard here? I bet you have."

"I'm still funnier, don't worry, but I've been trying to teach her," says Jeong lightly. His eyes remain tense. I wonder why (this time).

"Good, very good," says Ivanov. He keeps his smile plastered on, but it's the emptiest smile I've ever seen. His eyes are pretty red, too. Maybe it's because it's so late at night, and he just drove up from Boston. But maybe not.

Are all the bosses in the FBI creeps? I just hope Ivanov won't turn out like Marsters did.

"Anyway," I say. "Where's Benazir Allard? Did you stick her in one of these cells already?"

Jeong says, "Yes, but—"

"Can I see her?" I ask. "I want to check in with her. I promise I'll be careful."

"That's out of the question," says ASAC Ivanov crisply. "The specimen is about to be transported to our permanent research facility in Back Bay. Along with the other two specimens spawned from Katherine Marsters's adventure into World 72."

That's too many novel details for me to take in all at once. I try to work backwards. "Uh, World 72? Do you guys *know* the place that the Port led to? Or are you just in the habit of colonizing new dimensions with your own classification system?"

"That information is beyond what a civilian is permitted to know, Allard," Ivanov says.

"Because if the name's not settled on, I could make a

strong case for 'Graham's World,'" I go on. "Or 'Tsoukalasville,' if you don't mind a spelling challenge. Kid did the heavy lifting for you, the least you can—"

Jeong says, "Allard, shut up."

I look at him, surprised. He sounds scared. And this is the guy who stood up to not just one but three Kat Marsterses simultaneously. "Ethan," I say gently, "I don't need to be managed. I don't want to cause any friction between you and your superior here, but—I won't be cut out of the loop." I turn back to Ivanov. "I *went* to your World 72. I think I'm *permitted* to know a lot of fucking things."

"Keep this up," Ivanov says coldly—while still smiling, somehow! "—and I'll pack *you* into our permanent research facility too. Go ahead. You're halfway to convincing me. Who knows what contaminants you carried over from an unauthorized dimension? Who knows what alterations you yourself may have gone through while birthing your own clone?"

I respond in a small voice, "I wouldn't call it a *birthing* . . . my vagina was in no way involved in the phenomenon."

But I hurry to add, "Listen, you can't just put her in some secret facility—I want to know where she's heading and how I can get there. She's fucked up, but I promised I wouldn't abandon her."

Ivanov says, "How touching! Making vows to an extradimensional murderer. I'm afraid we can't be held responsible for those vows, though." He gestures at one of the cells. "We're taking her and the two Marsters specimens to Boston. To be thoroughly examined. The research possibilities with these specimens are tremendous. The testing I can imagine is . . . nearly *infinite*. And if their exteriors prove to be unremarkable, well, we'll at least make an effort to examine their insides."

Benazir shouldn't be excused for her crimes, of course. She should face punishment, and captivity. At least long enough for scientific minds to explore the possibility of psychological improvement and redemption. Maybe she's flooded with some kind of rage chemical that could be toned down. In that sense, I support the research aspect. But Ivanov isn't talking about that. He's talking, clearly, about torture. Not to mention dissection.

That's not an appropriate punishment in any lawbook *I've* ever heard of. Not in the United Fucking States of America. Call me naïve, but I'm going to insist on going by the book, even for hateful little doppelgängers. Even for the two Evil Marsterses, if I'm going to be ethically consistent.

My anger boils up. This time, I'm not going to hold it back.

"I *won't* let you do that," I say.

Jeong says, "Allard, *please*. You're gonna get yourself in a lot of trouble."

"Et tu, Ethan?" I snap at him. "Guess I forgot what badge you're wearing."

"Ah!" says Ivanov. "There's that infamous anger I keep hearing about. I feel so privileged to witness it."

Jeong leans close and speaks low to me. "Just stop— there's nothing you can do here."

I block the door to Benazir's cell. "Stand down," I say to ASAC Ivanov. "Leave her here—and Marsters's twin minions, too. Do whatever kind of observing you like from here, but I refuse to let you take them down to Boston."

The agent just shakes his head, still unnaturally smiling, and pulls his weapon on me. I unfortunately returned Jeong's Glock 26 to him back at the Sheafe Warehouse, so I'm unarmed. And I don't have the "biplanar" key I'd need to spring Benazir myself.

I guess I figured it would end like this. Now I just need to decide if I'm ready to die to protect a murderous doppelgänger. Everything about this is wrong. In my cop-era daydreams, if I sacrificed myself nobly to save someone else, that someone was usually a child, a kindly grandma, or a hot redhead.

Then Jeong clubs me from behind with the butt of his Springfield, and I go down.

"I have to say," the ASAC says, as McGuinness and Barnes hurry in to check out the commotion, "she's making this next part a whole lot easier on my conscience."

His words sound soupy. I was already tired and off balance. Now, with a new blow to the head, I need all my energy just to interpret what he's saying. However, he's not talking to me.

Agent Jeong kneels and handcuffs me. "Just remember, you promised she won't actually be found guilty."

"I never promised you that," Ivanov says. "The vagaries of the American court system are beyond even my control. All we can do is try to improve the odds."

17

I mutter something unintelligible even to me as Jeong and McGuinness haul me to my feet. Not roughly, at least there's that.

"Put her in a cell, please," Ivanov says. "We've got to arrange the transfer of the specimens first. Plus, if we hold off on turning Allard over to the police for a few hours, we'll get a greater amount of news coverage."

News coverage. Their plan for me is coming into focus through the haze. Don't I feel like an idiot right now for trusting anyone, anyone at all.

The FBI agents open up the door to the right of Benazir Allard's cell and escort me inside. It may be a steel cage, but it is at least nicer than the holding cell back at the Portsmouth PD. For one thing, the bed is a bed, not a shelf, and though it's small, it looks soft. There's even a pillow this time. The toilet in the corner is sadly lacking a roll of paper, though.

"Sorry about this, Divya," Jeong says. He removes my handcuffs as McGuinness stands guard by the door. Then he digs in my pockets and takes my wallet, keys, smartphone, and Graham's sketchbook. "May not seem like it now, but this'll all work out for you in the end."

"And what about Benazir?" I ask him softly. "How will this work out for her?"

He looks at me, and for a brief instant his old good humor shines through. Talk about an inopportune time for it. "Don't worry about her. You have my personal guarantee she won't be abused, dissected, drawn and quartered, or whatever else that asshole was talking about. This is the United States of America. We don't *do* that."

"Bullshit. *Bullshit,* Ethan. Ever hear of Abu Ghraib?"

Jeong's mouth sets in a hard line. "Just try to be thankful you're alive."

"Oh, and I'm out of TP," I go on. "Be sure to write out a copy of your 'personal guarantee' so I can wipe my ass with it."

Shaking his head, Jeong leaves the cell, and McGuinness closes it behind him.

My head's still pounding. And I'm so tired, and frustrated. I lie back on the cot. It's as comfortable as I hoped. From what Ivanov said, I won't be staying here long, so I'd be smart to grab some z's while I can. However, I find that I can't just fall asleep. I keep thinking about the woman on the other side of the wall.

Eventually I call out: "Benazir. Can you hear me?"

"Not my name," comes the faint reply through the wall.

"Just wanted to say . . . I'm sorry. I tried to help you. But I guess I'll be breaking my promise after all."

"Big surprise," says the woman with my voice. "Color me shocked. I won't hold it against you—I'll just think of all the good times we've had instead."

I'm out of energy, and out of patience for my own

sarcasm. I roll over on the the cot and try to sleep. I don't dream, which is a small mercy.

Agent Barnes shakes me awake. It's impossible to tell how many hours have passed without any windows or a watch or my smartphone. The woman looks down at me with a pitying expression.

"Morning, Divya," she says. "It's time to face your public."

I DON'T KNOW when all the media started to arrive. Maybe last night, sometime when I was sleeping. Maybe during the tail end of my nocturnal adventures and I just didn't notice them parachuting in. In any case, every major media outlet that I can think of is here. Big news network shows, national publications, news and gossip websites, everyone's got a reporter and a cameraman here. They're all shoving their microphones and lenses in my face at the same time.

"Why did you kill your old friends in the police force? Why now?"

"What were you thinking as you were ending Eric Kuhn's life?"

"Does your family have a history of mental illness, or are you the only one?"

"What can you tell us about the rumors you have a twin sister?"

It's a rehash of the dark days of last year—except so much worse. The news outlets are so much bigger than before, and so much more insistent. Not only did a college student with rumored kinky sex habits die mysteriously last night, but then a news reporter got his brains bashed out, and four died and several suffered wounds in an unprecedented assault on the local police station. Portsmouth hasn't seen this much violence since its founding fathers wiped out the Wabanaki and worked African slaves into an early, unmarked grave.

"*This sleepy seaside town is shocked by the gruesome events of yesterday evening . . .*"

"*Residents of this tourist magnet on the New Hampshire Seacoast feel anger, fear, and disgust over the murders and wanton destruction allegedly wreaked by a former member of the Portsmouth Police Department, disgruntled by her dishonorable dismissal last year . . .*"

"*Many questions remain unanswered this morning as this tiny port city wakes up to blood running in its quaint streets . . .*"

The bastards prattle on and on into their cameras as if they could tell their Piscataqua from their Winnacunnet. They claim to have the truth, or to be pursuing the truth, while they're busy concocting their own version. Just like before, the many wear the cloak of journalism that belongs, in truth, to only a few—all while pushing their own narratives, their own viewer hooks, their own fresh opportunities for massive advertising revenue.

I ignore them all. Whatever Barnes and Jeong might have been instructed, they choose to interpret their task as chivvying me through the media crowds as quickly as possible.

When we finally get inside the car and shut out the media's ravenous din, nobody says a word. I can't even look Jeong in the eye—I don't know how he can live with himself, setting me up as the fall girl for my doppelgänger's crimes. Does he accept it as part of the job, even after all I did to chase Benazir down and eliminate the threat of the Port? Or is he just too scared for his own job to defy Ivanov?

Maybe more than a demotion's at stake. Maybe Ivanov is

the type who can make people disappear. Jeong did tell me: *Just try to be thankful you're alive.*

Even so, I can't forgive Jeong. I can't forgive any of them. If I make it out of this alive, I promise I'll never ally myself with these two-faced Feds ever again.

They drive me to the Rockingham County Jail, over in Brentwood. It's a dour brick facility surrounded by plenty of concertina wire. As Jeong and Barnes prepare to hand me off to the corrections officers, I break the silence: "I helped you guys solve the murder of Graham Tsoukalas. It was his own Port-spawned twin; case closed. I was promised information about Hannah's death in return, but all I got was Marsters telling me that the Port cultists must have murdered her. I need names. I need *evidence*. Where is it?"

Barnes says unhappily, "ASAC Ivanov anticipated you would ask about that. He said to tell you that you made a deal with Kat Marsters, not with the agency as a whole. Sorry, Divya. We have nothing to tell you."

"*You must know something,*" I say, with more than a twinge of desperation. "What did *you* guys hear about Hannah Ryder's death at the time? What have you heard in the time since? Does the blame fall on the cultists, or is that bullshit?"

"We don't have that information," Jeong says.

"I know Hannah was in the Tenacious Trainers," I press. "Did she have a fight with any of the other members? Anyone with a red winter coat? *Please.* You can't leave me to rot in here without a fucking clue!"

Jeong sighs. He opens his mouth, about to tell me *something*. But Agent Barnes elbows him, and so what Jeong says is: "Be safe, Allard. Have faith that you'll make it out to continue your own investigation."

A new figure enters the room: that famous champion of

justice, Attorney Barb Okefor, whom I last saw cowering behind a desk at the Portsmouth police station. The agents leave. And I get my new orange duds and an anti-suicide blanket as I'm processed into the custody of the jail to await my court date.

AS IT TURNS OUT, that court date never arrives. The testimony against me, the supposed murderer of four cops and a newspaper reporter, collapses before the prosecution can present their case. Turns out most of the police officers who witnessed the slaughter keep talking some crazy story about Divya Allard having a sister or cousin, maybe a Muslim terrorist from Pakistan or something, who looked *just* like her and was responsible for the shooting. These police officers describe Divya Allard as actually stopping this nefarious relative from killing anyone else.

Chief Akerman, the most credible witness, denies all of this and places the blame for the murders squarely on me. But Akerman is outnumbered by the other officers: Milly Fragonard, Rick McLaren, Ben Ulrich (surprisingly!), and Kate Haring.

I'm glad to know that, though they may not be friends of mine, there are still honest, incorruptible cops in the Portsmouth force. I'd been beginning to lose hope. But the chief heartlessly flipping on me is cause for concern.

And as for the murder of Eric Kuhn in Prescott Park? The assailant left no DNA behind, and the only two witnesses disagree on what they saw. Upstanding citizen Margaret Shaw saw me killing the reporter. Not-so-upstanding citizen Solomon Shrive saw not me, but . . . this insane terrorist relative all those cops were talking about. Who knew?

So I walk out of the Rockingham County Jail a free woman. It's early June. I haven't missed much in the world except for a progression in the blooming of trees and flowers. The brief spring of New England has paved the way for the long summer.

Oh, I *did* miss Wallace Riggs and Neria Francoeur getting cleared in the matter of Graham Tsoukalas's death. I'm still not sure how it happened. But I have an idea.

Given the swift action of Agent Ethan Jeong, it was the FBI, not the local police, who found the second body of Graham Tsoukalas in the dumpster behind the Tenacious Trainers gym. So the FBI grabbed Evil Graham's body and trundled it off to their special research facility down in Back Bay, to join the growing collection of clones dead and alive from Graham's World (I will *not* call it "World 72").

The local police and the media, ignorant of that body, missed the opportunity to entertain another evil twin/relative story. Thus the FBI could have framed Wallace and Neria for the crime, just as they made me the patsy for Benazir's kills. But they were missing the juicy element that could have sealed the deal: the salacious DVD. Thank God I'd handed it off to Sol. The FBI had no motive to pin on those two, since nobody but me and Mrs. Tsoukalas knew that Graham had been sex partners with Wallace and Neria.

Graham Tsoukalas's murder remains unsolved, therefore. And, of course, the murders of Daniels, Piotrowski, Berger, Bradley, and Kuhn. But in those latter cases, public opinion knows who the real culprit is.

Me.

Even though I'm innocent, these legal shenanigans have permanently stained what little reputation I had left. I got a

call at the jail yesterday from Mr. Baldini at Jacobi Investment Associates. Turns out I'm out of a job. Once again. The
partners at JIA were eager to shed all association with me,
and almost fired Mr. Baldini too for his poor judgment
hiring me in the first place. I felt bad for the guy; Mr. Baldini
was almost crying as he told me. I think he didn't buy into
the charges against me. I'm pretty sure, anyway.

I told him not to worry: I'll be able to land on my feet
somehow. I've got friends who can help me. All the usual
comforting lies, etc. Plus I promised I'd still stop by to
discuss football scores.

Truth is, I don't how I'm going to keep my apartment.

They hand me an unmarked envelope along with my
personal effects as I walk back into my life of freedom.
Outside the jail, a small group of people with signs has gathered to protest my release. *KILLER COP WALKS — WHY?*
And *LOCK HER UP! NO TO RADICAL ISLAM!* (I'm Hindu,
but thanks for lumping me in with Osama Bin Laden.
Brown people are all the same anyway, right?) And most
chilling of all, *WE'LL BE WATCHING YOU.*

Oh, I'm going to have a lot of people watching me in the
coming days and weeks and months of my life. I can count
on that.

I refraining from feeding the trolls. I walk by them,
ignoring their calls and their jeers. Someone throws an
orange at me—why is it always fruit with these hecklers?—
but I manage to dodge it. Seems that my reflexes didn't
atrophy while in prison.

I try to look on the bright side. It's a beautiful day in the
beautiful Seacoast. And I do have one friend waiting for me.
Mr. Sol Shrive, ne'er-do-well server at the Friendly Toast,
has brought my car to Brentwood for me. We hug and he
hops into the shotgun seat.

"You okay?" he says.

I settle behind the wheel and take a deep breath.

"Now I am," I say. "But a few ladies back in the penal system are really gonna miss me."

"Whoa!" Sol says, grinning. "You dog!"

"Sadly, not in that way. But thanks for your everlasting faith in my libido." I open the envelope I was handed at checkout. There's a brief note inside:

Benazir is safe in Boston. Let's talk. — SSA Jeong

Looks like Ethan has gotten himself a promotion, thanks to his years of service and loyalty to the agency. Unfortunately for him, we have nothing to talk about. I crumple the note and throw it out the window, then I pull away from the jail and head back to Portsmouth.

"You hungry? You must be," my friend says. "You gotta try the breakfast burritos at Dos Amigos. It's a new addition to their menu. You've missed a lot, but I'll help you catch up."

I laugh. "You act like I was locked up for years, Sol. I don't need any 'readjustment' to life outside the big house, thank you very much. I just need information—what did the Tenacious Trainers say when you went back to them?"

Glancing at him, I notice for the first time that Sol *looks* different. There's a new energy dancing in his eyes. Sol picks up on my scrutiny and averts his gaze, looking out the window instead. "They . . . showed me things. Divya, that Port in the Sheafe Warehouse was only the barest beginning. You wouldn't believe what these people have been up to."

"Do they seem capable of murder?" I ask artlessly.

Sol shakes his head slowly. "They're seekers. Travelers. You have to meet them, Divya. They certainly want to meet you."

I've had a lot of time to cool my heels and unpack what exactly happened on that long, insane night in May. I'd figured out early on that the Tenacious Trainers were the ones who placed the anonymous call to me about the death of Graham, their brother in Port-chasing. But it took me longer to realize why they called me—it wasn't *just* because of my relationship with you.

"You know what?" I say. "I think I already *have* met at least one of them."

"Huh?"

I ignore his bewilderment and press on: "Why do they want to meet with me? I already helped them figure out what happened to Graham."

"They want to help you in return," Sol says.

I reflect on the results of my last alliance. The FBI let me do the dirty work, find out the truth behind Graham's murder, and the truth of the Port as well, and even let me close it myself. And then they set me up as the fall girl for Benazir's crimes. Sure—it was technically my own careless-ness that caused those crimes in the first place. I'll forever carry the deaths of Kuhn and the four cops on my conscience. But that doesn't mean I'll ever forgive Jeong and the rest of those double-crossing Feds.

"I would prefer to work alone," I say.

"Understandable!" says Sol. "But don't you want to look them in the eye and determine for yourself what they're capable of?"

I sigh.

"Good," he goes on. "How about tonight? They're very eager. And, um, I was planning to meet them tonight anyway. I've decided—I want to be initiated. I'm going to get the wrist device."

Briefly I wonder at the wisdom of the path I've set Sol

on. Those wrist implants seem to invite a higher mortality rate than I'm comfortable with. But he's an adult, and he's in the program, and he can make decisions for himself. I stare at the road ahead and say, "Set it up. And I'll set a course for breakfast burritos."

18

N ew Castle, the rich Republican enclave of an island just off the coast of Portsmouth, seems like an unlikely place to meet scruffy radical cultists obsessed with other dimensions. Then again, maybe that's why they chose it for a meeting spot.

Evening drapes itself over the Seacoast as I walk to my appointment. I make my way up the hill to South Street and then head down New Castle Road. The water of the harbor stretches over on my left, restless and dark. I can see the old naval prison across the water. It reminds me of my recent incarceration; I shudder. *Never again.*

A series of bridges connects the mainland with the island of New Castle. In between the bridges lie a few lumps of land with their own access to the water. I step off the road at one of these spots and scramble down the sandy hill to the rocky beach area. A night fisherman sits on a half-submerged rock close to me, but he only gives me a glance before returning to his casting, his headlamp shining on the water. At the far end of the beach I see a small group of dark figures chatting in low voices.

I shine my flashlight on them. My lurid expectations for the cult are quickly dashed: none of these folks are wearing hoods or robes, nor is there a glass of Kool-Aid in sight. The first face I recognize is Sol's; he gestures at me to turn the light out, but I ignore him. Then I see a tall, brown-skinned guy with his arms folded, looking at me with complacent calm. He barely squints at my light. Finally, there's a dark-haired man and a blonde woman standing close together and conferring. They break their conversation as the light hits them, and the woman says, "Off."

Initially this couple puts me in mind of Wallace and Neria. I'm not sure why: the two couples couldn't be more different. Regarding Graham Tsoukalas's hapless friends, Wallace was very much the dominant figure physically, while Neria was slender, almost wispy. Here, the woman is the taller, more muscular one, while the man is thin, with bad posture, seeming to fold up on himself. Maybe he's not as short as he looks, but the woman is definitely the more noticeable physical presence. Fit and gorgeous. Looks like only one of these two is actually using the equipment at the Tenacious Trainers gym.

The man with bad posture has a pleasant face from closer up. Glasses, freckles. He's even younger than her; he looks fresh out of college or still enrolled. He's folded up because he's reading a book on an e-reader. I see that he has a wrist gadget.

I know the blonde woman, of course. She was leading the 3Peters' protest against the construction of the Seafare Estates on that tense afternoon (and nearly got shot by Officer Lewis). But I knew to expect her here before I stepped onto this beach. Tonight it's clear that she has a wrist device like the other cultists; she's wearing a form-fitting red sweater with the sleeves rolled up. I have a brief mental image of exploring that body from head to toe. Then I shake off the vision, disgusted with myself. *Not* the time.

"I said, 'off,'" the woman repeats.

I'm not usually one for following commands. I keep my light on her and say, "So, I figured out you'd be the one waiting for me. Sol mentioned that a woman around his age tried to recruit him into the Trainers. You fit the bill age- and physique-wise, and I never forgot the intensity in your eyes. You also told me I'd have to 'pick a side' someday, a phrase only used by the truly persecuted—or people who *believe* themselves to be."

"Brava, Allard," she says. "Now would you please?"

I relent and direct the flashlight onto the sand, where it'll still provide ambient illumination. "What I still haven't quite cracked is why you threw in with the 3Peters to protest the new condo building. With your eye on other worlds than this, surely you can't care all that much about afford-able housing or a communal water view. What's your real issue with the Seafare Estates construction? They build it right over one of your Ports?"

I'm half-joking as I say this last part, but the shocked look on the young woman's face tells me I've hit the target.

However, she recovers quickly and says, "I have common cause with anyone brave enough to challenge the rich and powerful in this city. That's all you need to know about *that*. I thought you'd want to discuss more important topics, like the untimely deaths of mutual friends."

Few questions so far, mostly commands and statements. She's used to getting what she wants. I can play this too.

"Name," I say.

The woman heaves an impatient sigh. She offers me her hand. "Nadia Chopin," she says. "Pleased to *officially* meet you."

She has, unsurprisingly, a firm grip. I withdraw my hand and check that all my little fingers are still there.

"And I'm, uh, Trig," says the kid, hastening to join us, though still holding onto his e-reader. I look in his eyes. He doesn't seem particularly *fervent*. Doesn't seem like he'd blow up a mall.

I check Nadia's eyes once again with this criterion in mind. No killer instinct there either. But her gaze is certainly full of intelligence, with an ironic glint.

"You were the one who called me," I say, pointing at Trig. "Anonymous Caller, the night Graham died."

He nods but says nothing. Nadia's the one who answers. "As soon as we heard about Graham's death, I thought of you. You'd shown your integrity that same afternoon. Keeping that cop from threatening me. You had no reason to help me, but you did it anyway."

"But if *you* called me, I'd recognize your voice right away," I say.

"Wouldn't make for much of an anonymous call," she agrees.

The kid's attention drifts back down to his e-reader. Either he's expecting her to do all the talking, or he just can't resist a good book. I target him with a: "Hey, whatcha reading?"

He looks up with a guilty expression. "*Dance of Numbers.* It's—well, you wouldn't have heard of it, probably. Specialized."

So far the tall guy hasn't said a word, and nobody's made a move to introduce him. With his arms folded, I can't tell if he has a wrist device too.

"You helped us out," Nadia says to me. "We're inclined to help you in return. And to offer you a lot more, if you're interested."

I wait for clarification, without asking for it. I get the inkling Nadia is used to manipulating people.

"I wonder if you would come with me first," she finally says. "I've got a lot to tell you, but I'd rather not tell you *here*."

"Then why did you want to meet me here?" I ask impatiently.

"Oh, we don't have far to go." She nods at Trig, who produces a plastic bottle of water from his shoulder bag and hands it over. The other cultists—or Tenacious Trainers, however I should think of them—clear the area around her, and Nadia takes a few steps back and then uncaps the bottle and flings a few drops into the air. Then she starts pacing a circular path in the sand and rocks, while speaking a string of unintelligible, wet syllables. She flings more water at the same spot in the air.

"Oh, no," I say, "not again. *No!*"

Startled, Nadia breaks off her movement and arcane speech, and the shimmering that has begun to wrinkle the night air now fades. "What? What's the problem?"

Sol reaches for me in a placating fashion, but I swat him away. I snap at Nadia: "You know what the problem is. We went through hell to close the *last* Port you people opened."

Finally the tall man speaks up. His accent is strange, silken. "The Ports aren't all the same," he says. "Graham Tsoukalas was reckless. He went on his own, didn't know what he was doing or where he was going. He chose poorly. This one—trust me. It's safe."

"Safe?" I say indignantly. "And who the hell are you?"

"I'm Durmaz IN of Stroyer's Axle," the man responds. "This Port leads to my home."

~

I'VE BEEN STUNNED into silence. But my eyes still function, so I rove them over this man calling himself Durmaz IN. He looks human enough—sure, a tall and thin specimen with a rather elongated face, but there's nothing unusual about him. Well, scratch that. He *is* unusually pretty. His brown skin is lustrous, and his thick black hair shines blue in the faint moonlight (is he a desi too?). If I were into men, I'd probably want to fuck him.

But as Durmaz self-consciously fidgets with his hair under my scrutiny, he draws attention to his ears—which are *pointed* at the top. And for the first time I notice the unusual device hanging over one of his ears and extending a small wire to near his mouth. It's golden and filigreed with fine, lace-like detail. Won't find that at Radio Shack.

No. Not gonna let a pair of fake ears and a newfangled earpiece fool me. "Bullshit."

Durmaz gives me a bland smile.

"We didn't invent the wrist implants, Allard," Nadia says. "They come from another world—Durmaz's world. And that's where we're going to take Sol to get his own implanted tonight."

Sol nods eagerly. "They're not just, like, heart rate monitors. They allow the Trainers to communicate with and locate each other, and, well . . . they're how you find Ports! You get a vibration in your wrist when there's one near."

I'm still not sure I'm ready to accept any of this, particularly the part about a cross-dimensional being standing right in front of me and speaking English. But before I met Benazir, I would have dismissed her as impossible too.

Still assessing the situation, I look at the Tenacious Trainers, and the supposed foreigner, and my friend Sol. It's cold here on the little beach, with the darkness and the pre-summer wind. The water in the harbor is swift-moving and deep; I wonder what secrets it holds underneath the surface, just like the city itself seems to hold.

I'm having trouble not feeling bitter about the fact that you hid all this from me. You committed yourself to this secret club and got your decoder ring—sorry, Port-sensing wrist thing—and you didn't want to tell me about it? Maybe you were going to, eventually, and never got the chance. But if you'd hung around the Tenacious Trainers long enough for them to initiate you, that meant there was plenty of time for you to open up to me. Instead, you let that time slip away.

"Did you make her swear to secrecy?" I ask. "Did you make her promise not even to tell me?"

Nadia doesn't have to ask who I'm talking about. Instead, she says: "Is that what you want to hear?"

"Hey," Sol puts in. "There's no call for being mean, Nadia."

I relent. "Okay, just forget it. Whether you asked her to or not, Hannah must have had a good reason for keeping all of this from me."

"She did," Nadia says. "However much she may have loved you, you were a cop. And the Portsmouth police aren't our friends. Over the last couple of years, we've lost several of our members to opioid overdoses—people who had no drug problems before they died."

"No drug problems *you* knew about," I say. "Addiction can happen to anyone, trust me." I don't mean for my eyes to slide over to Sol at that point, but they do. He cringes.

Nadia lets out an angry cough. "I knew them. I knew them all. The circumstances were beyond suspicious in every case. But every time, your old colleagues would just look the other way—or worse."

"That's . . ." I struggle for words. "That's a hell of an accusation."

"And yet you were willing enough to believe in a department-wide conspiracy when your fiancée died," Nadia says. "Do you think this is any different? You saw how the police chief, Akerman, was willing to put you away for the crimes your doppelgänger committed. Sure, there are some honorable cops in the mix. But Prince, Lewis, Gomez? Somehow one of them always seemed to be involved, whenever one of these supposed OD cases turned up. I wouldn't trust them to investigate a parking ticket."

I know the guys she's referring to. None of them are good cops. Dirty, I can believe. But accomplices to murder, or even murderers themselves? That's going to take me a minute to process. "Then why keep doing this, if you could get killed at any moment?"

"Hm," Nadia says. Her intense gaze is on me. "Why didn't Jeanne d'Arc just throw her sword down and move to Poland? Why didn't Magellan just turn around and head home at the first thundercloud?"

I choose not to reply to this rather self-aggrandizing line of questioning.

She goes on: "An infinite number of other dimensions and universes are waiting for us. Some are scary, yes, as you've experienced—but a far greater number of them are beautiful. *Revelatory*, even. We can advance the human race by finding these other places, and traveling to them."

"What if you open the wrong door? And can't close it again?"

Nadia's eyes narrow. "That's always the objection and the fear. But we can't let ourselves be ruled by fear if there's a chance for transcendence. Look at what our government does: develop horrible weapons out of its own self-interest, weapons that if used against our own country would cause its utter destruction. And yet the government *doesn't hesitate* to keep researching new weapons of ever greater magnitudes of horror. What if we could commit to fearlessness in the pursuit of peace and spiritual ascension, instead of war and dominance?"

Sol is nodding along. But of course this is the same guy who says he can literally hear Portsmouth talking to him when he goes for a walk.

"I'd love to see the beautiful and transcendent places in the multiverse, or whatever," I say. "But not if it means releasing a bunch of monsters into our world before you *find* those places. You know? Just because the U.S. government takes insane, deadly risks, doesn't mean the rest of us need to."

Nadia breathes a sigh through her nose. "Just—let me show you. Don't interrupt this time."

She's finally worn me down. If this is what it'll take to understand what happened to you—and what motivated you to get entangled with these zealots in the first place—then I ought to shut my dumb mouth and give Nadia a shot. I show her my palms and step backward, and she begins the opening ritual once more.

Soon a furious rushing stream of water circles a patch of the air, and a window to another place comes into being.

I hear a car driving over the bridges behind us. Headlights sweep over and past us. "Not worried about witnesses?"

Trig clucks his tongue in dismissal. "People see what they want to see."

Suddenly I remember the night fisherman sharing the little beach with us. I turn back; he's still focused on his task, or at least it seems that way. Then he nods at me. "Ah," I say. "I'm sure your sentry helps, too."

Trig smiles and pushes his glasses up his nose.

"Detective Allard," Nadia says. The young woman extends her hand to me. Behind her, the Port roils, and—I don't know what I see beyond. It feels as wrong as the temple of the giant slug did.

OK. It was a mistake to think of Graham's World. I feel my limbs freezing in place. I shake my head.

"This one won't create a copy of you," she assures me. "It won't harm you, or the good people of Portsmouth, in any way. Trust me."

Met with my silence, she adds, "Please."

I haven't forgotten the terror of dislocation and the menace of those twinned serpents. But neither have I forgotten how I crossed through the last Port with you in my mind and heart. I'll look to you for strength once again.

"Okay," I say finally to Nadia Chopin, "but you first."

Nadia leans through head first rather than stepping through. She somehow pulls herself the rest of the way, with her legs dangling curiously in mid-air before crossing. Sol goes next, using the same method.

When I approach the Port myself, I see why they've chosen this awkward method of crossing: there's nothing to step *onto* on the other side. I see a curved far wall of gleaming metal but not much else. Cautiously, I stick my head through the Port, closing my eyes as if I'm about to plunge underwater. I feel an unpleasant tingling in my head and shoulders, similar to the experience of crossing through the warehouse Port.

I dare to open my eyes. A wave of disorientation hits me immediately because I'm facing *forward* when I should be facing down. I'm looking at the concavity of a shiny steel(?)

wall—floor?—that just goes on and on, above my head and sheer to the other side of the large room. Nadia and Sol are picking themselves up to stand on the wall or floor. We appear to be inside a big, hollow sphere. But my now-upright companions are standing parallel to my body, which should not be possible in relation to my legs and feet still perpendicularly planted on the sand back on Earth.

I snatch my head back into the world I know, treating myself to another gate-crossing brain zap, and I fall back on my ass in the sand, breathing heavily. Durmaz ɪN looks down at me kindly. "You don't want to do *that* for too long at a time. Hang between two universes. It'll break your head."

I nod, still unable to speak.

He walks over with curiously heavy steps and offers me a hand up. I accept. Then Durmaz adds, "So are you in or out? Just so you know, I was planning on heading in after you. Have to catch up with my family."

I let go of the man. I can tell he thinks I'm going to wuss out, and that pisses me off. I snap at him, "Hold my beer," and I put my head down like a bull and I launch myself through the Port at a charge.

Another zap and then I'm flying up, up above Nadia and Sol's alarmed faces, with far more momentum than I would have expected. I'm soaring toward an object floating in the center of the sphere. It's a statue, made of a similar metal to the sphere itself, but cast in blue—but what it's depicting, I haven't the faintest idea. Some kind of smaller sphere with a few dangling things at the bottom of it. Somehow I haven't stopped moving: gravity doesn't seem to have much of a say here, wherever *here* is. As I get closer, I can discern that the sphere of the statue is grated, allowing a look inside at a messy nightmare of sea creatures squashed together around a ravenous-looking, toothy mouth. The part that's dangling from the bottom of the statue sphere depicts a clownish, unsettling face set onto a neck of eels or lampreys, with two large fish opening their mouths to reveal human-like hands.

I slow to an unwelcome proximity to the weird statue and fling out my hands, though I'm loath to touch it.

"Allard!" Nadia calls up. "Launch yourself off the statue, to the far wall. That's where the door to the city is anyway. We'll meet you there."

City?

My fingers grasp the statue's grating. The merry face at the bottom seems to be leering at me. I ignore it and will myself to hand-over-hand my way to the backside of the statue. Then I let go and steady my feet firmly against the statue, half-expecting the contact to send the statue spinning in the opposite direction, toward the Port. But somehow it remains anchored in the air. I launch with violent force from the "artwork" and sail through space, approaching the curved wall, where I do indeed see the outline of a closed door or hatch now.

Too much force. I collide with the sphere wall, banging my shoulder at the point of impact. Sol heads for me in a series of light, deft leaps along the wall. He helps me, groaning, to my feet. "You okay, chief?"

"Good, I'm good," I say quickly. For whatever reason, I'm blushing as Nadia approaches in similarly lunar fashion, with Trig and Durmaz close behind. She gives me a sly smile.

"Never took you for an acrobat," Nadia says.

"You could have warned me about the—gravity here, asshole."

She takes my insult in stride. "Didn't want to spoil any surprises for you. The biggest one's coming right up."

"Wait," I say, as the woman tugs at the small handle on the door. "What is that thing in the middle?"

"Spirit of water," Nadia announces. The door pops open, letting in a surprisingly refreshing breeze. "We came through a water Port to get here."

"Doesn't look like a *spirit*," I say. "Looks like a monster." I think back to the Port to Graham's World. It was ringed with fire, and on the other side . . . "I saw a different monster in the place Graham found. Big slug. That supposed to be the 'spirit of fire?'"

She nods. "They're not monsters, though. They're, like, religious symbols. You'll understand all this, in time."

"Then . . ." I take a last look around the metallic sphere. "This is a temple, too. Just like the building that those twin serpent things destroyed in their attempt to get at me, in Graham's World." The religious connotations of *cult* strike me anew. "Who *built* them, then?"

Nadia waves a finger at me. "Try to focus your full attention on what's behind this door." She gestures for me to go through.

I frown at her. I think I've earned the right to be suspicious of everyone at this point. But I do go through, and I gasp at the fantastic city that meets my eyes.

Great towers and bridges and domes rise above me in shining abundance, all in gold like Durmaz's earpiece. But they aren't what immediately catches my gaze. No, it's the fact that out here, we seem to be inside *another* sphere: a titanic one, like a city-sized bubble, through which I see surging cerulean in all directions. Rising in front of me, in the middle of a kind of city park, is a great wheel-like mechanism enclosed in its own protective dome, with pipes and gears emerging from the dome and snaking to every corner of this metropolis—or so I assume, as I realize I'm only looking at part of the city, and that it is curved in a way to match the bubble sphere that encases it.

I step out into the park. Here gravity's much more like what I'm used to, though with still a barely detectable lighter touch than Earth's 1G. I take a couple of delightfully graceful strides and then look back. Above the metal sphere I see more skyscrapers and other proud urban phalluses reaching in the direction of the bubble.

From the curve of this city, I'm shocked to realize that it's anchored in the center of its bubble in much the same way the "spirit of water" was in the metal sphere, and that all the buildings are growing outward like a ball of golden spikes. Impossible.

"The Axle," Nadia says, gesturing at the mechanism in the dome. "It's why this place is called Stroyer's Axle. They use it to travel the world sea."

I barely hear her. I bounce along on the park grass, the crush of my excitement overtaking the slight gravitational boost and causing me to stagger. This isn't just some relic of a lost civilization, like the temple in Graham's World seemed to be. This is a living city. Durmaz is no fraud, no exception. There are *many* people here: walking through the park, moving in the windows of the towers, zooming around on scooter-like vehicles. All in lovely tones of brown, all of them far more attractive than little old me. And none of them seem to be paying us any particular mind, except for the two stationed outside the metal sphere I've just exited.

These two clasp hands with Durmaz, exchange a few words with him, and then talk with Nadia and Trig—and Sol, who, while appreciative of his surroundings, does not look *surprised* by this city. Clearly he's already been on this magical mystery tour; maybe it's the standard procedure for newbies. I turn my attention to examining the two locals—guards, if that's what they are.

Like Durmaz, the two men could pass for height- and beauty-advantaged humans. Their uniforms are azure and close-fitting, with an unfamiliar star-shaped logo over the heart. But they have the same point to their ears, the same weird ear-hanging device Durmaz does, and there's one other detail that would definitely draw stares if they were walking through Market Square: a kind of scope covers (or has replaced?!) their left eye, a circular, red-glassed device that would look right at home sitting on a sniper rifle.

"These visits really should be cleared with the navigator first," one of them says to Nadia. Again in English. It occurs to me the earpiece thing is a translator.

"We have an understanding . . ." Nadia begins to reply. My attention drifts back to the city itself, the sea pressing against the bubble, and the Axle in its dome. I walk toward the Axle with unsteady steps. And I can almost sense you walking beside me.

Had you *been* here?

If so—good gods, *why didn't you tell me*?

My mind is exploding right now with the implications of . . . this. This city. This world. Graham's World. People, civilizations, territories beyond everything I ever thought I understood. No wonder once someone crossed through a Port, they thirsted for more. How deeply did you thirst?

"They want to take this from us," says Nadia. She glides in front of me and takes my hand gently. In a daze, I don't resist. "There are *hundreds* of Ports in the city—in Portsmouth—and those are just the ones we know about. Trig estimates there may be thousands left to uncover. Think of the universes, the *multiverses,* waiting for us. It's the greatest discovery humanity has ever made!"

"Who's they?" I say numbly.

Nadia's already wound up; there's no stopping her. "But they don't want us to visit these places, and explore and learn. They want us—they want us *all,* including themselves —to be steeped in ignorance. They kill us to protect the status quo. They're rich and powerful and they like things just the way they are."

"Nadia," I snap. I know she's not talking about the police this time. I squeeze her hand harder until she draws it away. "Nadia. Who? Who's killing you?"

"You should know by now, Detective," she says, scowling at me and nursing her fingers.

I know she's manipulating me at least a little here. Making me speak the answer she's leading to—well, that just makes it seem like *my* idea, doesn't it? Classic. But it doesn't mean her answer is wrong. Portsmouth is full of wealthy stakeholders. Gates to other universes opening up willy-nilly in their city would certainly complicate their investments. Particularly if some of those universes are as dangerous as Graham's World proved to be. But there's only one group of stakeholders who could hold the police chief in the palm of their hands.

I was right all that time to suspect a vile conspiracy to cover up your death. I was simply wrong to think that it ended with Chief Akerman.

"The city council," I say, with the horrible weight of truth threatening to drive me into the ground. Lighter gravity be damned.

"Almost all the councilors have drenched their hands with blood," Nadia says, nodding. "But it was Councilor Stone who killed Hannah that night."

Stone. I think back to the elegant woman at the podium in front of the Seafare Estates. I have a hard time imagining her committing murder. But I don't doubt that she's capable of it. "How? Why?"

Nadia's gaze pierces through me. "I don't know exactly what Hannah was up to that night. But I believe she found a new Port. At the excavation site. I think she was going to open it when Stone killed her."

"Hannah used her wrist device to locate it," I say.

Nadia looks at me grimly. "That's right."

"How would Stone have known she was there at that moment?"

"I don't know," she admits. "The councilors have been trying to track us down. They must have ID'ed Hannah as a member of our organization. At first I assumed that *you* had found out, through your relationship, and ratted on her to your police chief. But you showed me pretty quickly how wrong I was. Getting yourself suspended and all."

I realize I've missed asking the obvious question. "How do you know Stone was the killer?"

"Because I saw her," Nadia says softly. "I was there that night."

I see tears brimming in the woman's eyes. The harsh façade she's built is finally crumbling. My heart lurches, and I take her hands again. "I—promise I won't squeeze this time." No matter how desperate I am for her to continue.

She accepts my comfort. She takes a hitching breath. "Hannah invited me to that spot, that night. I believe, I believe she wanted to show me a new Port. What else could it have been, out there? Hannah arrived first. But someone else got there before I did. It was dark and I don't think either of them saw me as I walked toward them . . . This other person, this woman, crept up behind Hannah. She was wearing a red coat with a hood, but she pulled the hood down just before she attacked Hannah."

Red coat. Oh shit. That detail never made it into the *Porthole.* I find I'm stroking Nadia's solid hands obsessively, and I force myself to stop. Nadia *was* there.

"It was Grace Stone. No doubt about it. She—" Nadia lets out a choking sob. "No, my god. Hannah was your fiancée. You don't want to—"

"Goddamn right I want to hear it," I murmur, though my own cheeks are wet now too. "I need to. Please."

She swallows. "Stone picked up a rock and she, she *beat* Hannah with it. First in the head, and then all over her poor body. Hannah was surprised and she never had a chance. When Hannah stopped moving, Stone shoved on her body until it rolled down into the pit. Then she pulled her hood back over her face and walked away."

"And so did you," I say.

My tone was flat, bereft of accusation, but Nadia flinches anyway. "Yeah," she whispers. "I was afraid. I'm—I'm sorry. I wanted to come to you and tell you what happened to her. So many times, I almost did. But I knew it would open up so many questions, and—and I couldn't. I didn't trust the police. I'd seen several of my friends disappear already. So what good would it even have done to tell you?" She pauses. "That's what I thought then, anyway. Now I know . . . I should have told you. I am so sorry."

The old Divya Allard might have judged Nadia more harshly for her actions. She had, after all, contributed to me spending months in a vortex of mental anguish and uncertainty. If Benazir were here, she'd surely urge me to slap this kid upside her pretty face.

But all I feel now is relief. Profound relief, like Nadia just shot an enema through my stopped-up soul. My stomach turns a little at my own internal choice of metaphor, so instead I focus on the gift that this woman has given me:

I know my enemy.

I now have Stone's name and face to focus my retributive energy, and I've never felt more energized before this moment. The golden wonders of the bubble-encased city collapse before me as my mind turns itself wholly to its new task.

"You were hoping she killed Graham Tsoukalas too," I say. "So that I'd collect the evidence against her that you lacked in the case of Hannah's murder. That's the real reason you turned to me."

Nadia purses her lips. "Yeah. I honestly thought Graham was another of her victims."

"Sorry to disappoint," I say. "But don't worry. One way or another, I'll find the evidence we need."

I let go of her and turn back to the metal sphere.

"Hey," Nadia calls after me. "Where are you going? I've got so much to show you here!"

"Later," I say. "Right now I've got a city council to destroy."

END OF BOOK 1

READY FOR THE NEXT BOOK?

City of Games: The Shadow Over Portsmouth Book 2
is available now on Amazon!

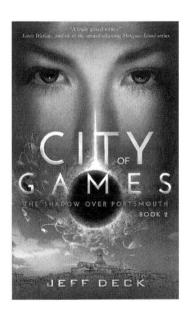

ACKNOWLEDGMENTS

Thank you to Kate Rocheleau, Abree Murch, and Kerry Doherty for their beta reads of several chapters of *City of Ports* and their many great ideas and suggestions for the book. Thanks as well to Marcelo Gallegos, Bryan Thompson, and Kali Moulton for providing illustrations of certain key figures in *The Shadow Over Portsmouth* mythos that helped me to better picture them in my own head. I'm grateful to Damonza for designing another excellent book cover (check out their work on *The Pseudo-Chronicles of Mark Huntley* cover as well).

Heartfelt thank yous and hugs to Cassie Gustafson, my accountability buddy during many sessions of drafting and editing this book (as well as other stories). It is an immense source of motivation and support to work in the same physical space as another writer. Speaking of those spaces, I have to give a shout-out to Adelle's Coffeehouse and Flight Coffee in Dover, and the Portsmouth Book & Bar, for being the spots where much of this story came into being, coaxed along by copious caffeine.

Thanks very much to Portsmouth Detective Rochelle

Navelski, former Portsmouth Police Chief Dr. Lou Ferland, and retired FBI Agent Ted Mahoney for providing me with crucial understanding and details of the Portsmouth Police Department and the FBI's Portsmouth Resident Agency office. Dr. Ferland also published a book, *Historic Crimes & Justice in Portsmouth, New Hampshire,* that is an incredible resource for learning about not just the history of the city's PD but also the city itself. The police department and FBI RA office portrayed in the book are in no way intended as a criticism of their real-life counterparts. Certain aspects have been changed for dramatic effect, and any blatant goofs or other errors are the fault of the author alone (yours truly).

I'm grateful for the support I've received from the Portsmouth Writers' Night Out community that meets monthly at the aforementioned Book & Bar. I also thank the New Hampshire Writers' Project for presenting a stage reading from an early version of the book in April 2016 at the Hatbox Theatre in Concord, New Hampshire. The audience offered helpful suggestions about Divya Allard as the character was voiced for the first time. Afterward, Masheri Chappelle gave me some great insights that helped to shape this character. The NHWP offers many valuable programs and assets for writers in New Hampshire and beyond: their website is www.nhwritersproject.org.

Thank you to Dan Szczesny and Plaidswede Publishing for publishing the first story related to *The Shadow Over Portsmouth* "canon," a short piece called "Making the Transition," which appeared in *Murder Ink 2: Sixteen More Tales of New England Newsroom Crime* in 2017. Those curious about the tale should read it *after* this book, as it contains minor spoilers for *City of Ports.*

Thanks to my mom, Jane, Tom & Ginny, Mary, and Burleigh for believing in this story from the beginning. Ask

Tom sometime about a short piece from several years ago featuring Solomon Shrive venturing into the tunnels underneath the city; it appears to have stuck in his mind . . .

Finally, I thank the real Portsmouth, New Hampshire, itself and all those who work to make it a vibrant place. You will note that I've used many real places and businesses in the story. The fictional version comes in for some knocks in this series, but let's call it tough love for a city whose potential stretches to worlds beyond. Take a walk around the real Portsmouth and peer into the hidden lanes and quiet corners for yourself. You never know what doors you might find.

— JEFF DECK, SOUTH BERWICK, MAINE, AUGUST 3, 2018

LIKED THIS BOOK?

Sign up for e-mail updates at www.jeffdeck.com and get a free e-book!

And be sure to check out my other titles!

THE PSEUDO-CHRONICLES OF MARK HUNTLEY

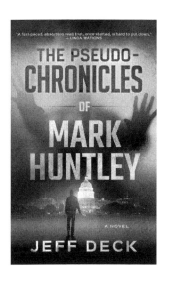

"Deck's writing is seamless and so natural that, as you become immersed in Huntley's increasingly bizarre world, you forget that the story is fiction. This is the mark of a truly gifted writer."
— Linda Watkins, author of the award-winning *Mateguas Island* series

MY NAME IS MARK HUNTLEY. All I really wanted to do was drink cheap beer and blog about my dead-end life. Then I stumbled across a secret war between two sinister alien forces. If I try to stop the war, I may get my friends and loved ones killed. If I don't try, the human race is toast. Oh yeah, and a demonic weapon inside me is probably driving me insane.

If I'm already dead when you find this, you need to carry on the fight.

THE PSEUDO-CHRONICLES of Mark Huntley is a blog mutated into a supernatural thriller. If you like the pulse-pounding terror of Stephen King and the smart, funny first-person storytelling of *The Martian*, you'll love meeting Mark Huntley. Find The Pseudo-Chronicles of Mark Huntley online, or request it at your favorite bookstore.

PLAYER CHOICE: AETHER GAMES,
BOOK 1

"Master game designer Glen Cullather is having the worst day of his life. Tough luck for him but great news for readers of PLAYER CHOICE. Its twisty plot and high-stakes action will thrill adventure fans, while its reality bending and speculation about the future of privacy will please admirers of the great Philip K. Dick. Check it out: Jeff Deck has got his game on." — James Patrick Kelly, winner of the Hugo, Nebula, and Locus awards

PLAYER CHOICE IS a fast-paced gaming sci-fi adventure that asks: What happens when unreality becomes our reality?

It's 2040. With neural implants, people can play games

in an immersive virtual reality known as the aether space. Game designer Glen Cullather has a plan for the most ambitious aether game ever imagined: a fantasy epic that gives players the freedom to do anything.

But Glen's own life is fragmenting into alternate realities. He can't tell whether his aether game idea has succeeded, or failed miserably. And Freya Janoske is either his biggest rival, or his most intimate partner. Glen must figure out what's real and what's, well, fantasy -- for his own survival! Find the e-book of Player Choice online. Print version coming soon.

ABOUT THE AUTHOR

 Jeff Deck is an indie author who lives in Maine with his wife, Jane, and their silly dog, Burleigh. Deck writes science fiction, fantasy, horror, dark fantasy, and other speculative fiction.

Deck is the author of *The Shadow Over Portsmouth* series (Book 1: *City of Ports*, Book 2: *City of Games*), the supernatural thriller novel *The Pseudo-Chronicles of Mark Huntley,* and the sci-fi gaming adventure novel *Player Choice*. He is also the author, with Benjamin D. Herson, of the nonfiction book *The Great Typo Hunt: Two Friends Changing the World, One Correction at a Time* (Crown/Random House). Deck is also a fiction ghostwriter and editor. He has worked with many authors to help them tell their own stories, and he has contributed content to a couple of video games.

In 2008, Deck took a road trip across the U.S. with friends to fix typos in signage and nearly wound up in federal prison. He enjoys reading speculative fiction, exploring New England with his family, playing video games, and plundering from the past and future.

facebook.com/jeffdeck

twitter.com/tealjeffdeck

instagram.com/jeffdeck

55964161R00128

Made in the USA
Middletown, DE
19 July 2019